Published by Bethany House Publishers
A Ministry of Bethany Fellowship, Inc.
11300 Hampshire Avenue South
Minneapolis, Minnesota 55438

Printed in the United States of America.

Library of Congress Cataloging-in-Publication Data

Shellenberger, Susie.
    Life, love, music, and money / Susie Shellenberger and Greg Johnson.
        p. cm. — (77 pretty important ideas on surviving planet earth)
    Summary: Offers advice with a Christian perspective on coping with a variety of emotional, spiritual, and social problems.
    ISBN 1-55661-485-3
    1. Teenagers—Religious life. 2. High school students—Religious life.
3. Teenagers—Conduct of life. 4. High school students—Conduct of life.
5. Christian life—Juvenile literature. Yl. Conduct of life. 2. Christian life."
I. Johnson, Greg. II. Title. III. Series: Shellenberger, Susie. 77 pretty important ideas.
BV4531.2.S47   1996
248.8'3—dc20   96-9943
                                        CIP
                                        AC

Life, Love, Music, and Money...

SUSIE SHELLENBERGER
& GREG JOHNSON

BETHANY HOUSE PUBLISHERS
MINNEAPOLIS, MINNESOTA 55438

77 Pretty Important Ideas

Lockers, Lunchlines, Chemistry, and Cliques
Cars, Curfews, Parties, and Parents
Camp, Car Washes, Heaven, and Hell
Life, Love, Music, and Money

Dedicated to

Greg and Shirley Lemerond

Thanks for fertilizing my lawn,

fixing my broken cabinet door,

and taking me on picnics.

But most of all . . . thanks for *you*.

—Susie Shellenberger

SUSIE SHELLENBERGER is the editor of *Brio* magazine for teen girls (cir. 160,000), published by FOCUS ON THE FAMILY. A graduate of SOUTHERN NAZARENE UNIVERSITY and the UNIVERSITY OF CENTRAL OKLAHOMA, Susie's experience with teens ranges from youth ministry to teaching high school speech and drama. She is the author of nine books, including *There's a Sheep in My Mirror* and *Straight Ahead.*

GREG JOHNSON is the former editor of *Breakaway* magazine for teen boys (cir. 90,000) and the author or coauthor of fifteen books, including *If I Could Ask God One Question* and *Daddy's Home.* A graduate of NORTHWEST CHRISTIAN COLLEGE, Greg has been involved with teens for over fifteen years and has worked with YOUTH FOR CHRIST and FOCUS ON THE FAMILY. He and his wife have two sons and make their home in Colorado Springs, where Greg is a literary agent for ALIVE COMMUNICATIONS.

 People DIE.

This one is kind of weird to start off with, we know, but it's absolutely HUGE to understand. Those who don't get a grip on death could forever be held in bondage to it.

Someone once described our bodies as "earthsuits." They were only meant to live in an oxygen/nitrogen atmosphere between certain altitudes. Hanging out under the water or thirty-six miles up (without proper equipment) definitely won't lead to a long and satisfying life. Further, if you disease, infect, shoot, crash, or otherwise grossly harm it . . . the earthsuit will probably expire. The body is fairly resilient, but **it's not bulletproof or cancerproof.**

The problem with death is that it rarely comes at a good time—whether you're the one who dies or the one who loses a loved one. This is the big problem for teens: **Death is never convenient!** For most, it's a painful interruption in a life that is otherwise uncomplicated. They feel they didn't do anything to deserve it (which is usually true); it hurts; it makes them think about their own mortality (for a day or two at least); and it generally is a major downer.

Plus, **it's scary.** Where do people go? If they're going to heaven, couldn't God have waited until they were older? After all, if eternity is ETERNITY, then what's the big hurry? If they're going to hell, God must really be a bad guy because He didn't give them one final chance to come to faith in Christ (you think).

There's not enough space to talk about this subject in a huge amount of detail, but one thing is sure: If you don't have the right theology (spiritual belief system) about death, you'll most likely live a tortured existence on Planet Earth. **You'll be angry at God** because you think it's His "job" to make sure your world never has any pain. And if you're angry at God, you're probably not going to want to get close to Him so He can show how your life can make a difference in this world . . . then you'll never really know that your life COULD have made a difference. Instead, you'll live for pleasure, yourself, material possessions, or other things that only last a short while.

Death IS emotionally painful. We are rarely ready for ourselves or a loved one to die. We must realize, however, that **life itself is a wonderful gift**—each comes with a lifetime guarantee. But we are not told how long that lifetime will be.

2 LEARN to be creative.

There are times when you'll *need* it . . . like on a hot summer day when there's absolutely nothing in the world to do because you've already ridden your bike, done the mall, gone camping, been to Bible study, listened to all your favorite CDs, driven past your empty school campus, memorized everything everyone wrote in your yearbook, browsed through the Yellow Pages, surfed through every TV channel in the galaxy, read this book twice, and called all your friends.

What else is there to do? Ahhh. This is where creativity comes in. We've all got it in us, even if we don't know it. Here's how it works:

Your brain is divided into two halves: the right and left side. Creativity involves using the right side of your brain. The left side is used for logic, gathering facts and compiling data, and making decisions. The right side is used for inventing, looking at things in a new way, color, and rhyme. We use both all the time without thinking about it.

One side or the other *does* tend to dominate, though. For instance, you may be more left-brained than right-brained. You might *think* you're not very creative because you're in the habit of exercising your left brain more. **You probably have just as much creativity as anyone else;** you're just not in the habit of making your right brain pull its own weight.

If you *are* a creative person, you may tend to think you're not very good at facts, numbers, or details. You *can* be! **It's just a matter of**

learning to think through situations and problems with your left brain in control.

Both halves of your brain are equally important. Learn to use them both effectively so that you can live up to your utmost potential.

Now . . . let your brain wander. **What could you do if you really put your mind to it?**

•Make the world's largest popsicle by filling an empty (and very clean) trash can or other large container with Kool-Aid, placing a 2 x 4 in the middle, and freezing it. What? Your freezer isn't that big? No sweat. Call your local ice house and ask them if you can put the world's largest popsicle in it for one night. Then call your friends and take pics of everyone eating chunks of your 45-pound grape frozen treat. Who knows? You may even make the local news or paper!

•Create your own water slide. All you need is a long piece of plastic or tarp. Lay it flat in your backyard, or an empty lot, and set the water hose on top of it. Turn on the H_2O, get a running start, and slide for miles (or however long your piece of plastic is).

•Play human bowling (sort of a variation on the water slide). Set up ten small plastic trash cans at the end of the tarp, get a good running start, and see how many you can knock down. You'll be the hit of your neighborhood.

•Write your own book. It's possible! Ever heard of the movie *The Outsiders?* Well, it started out as a book. And that book was written by seventeen-year-old Susan E. Hinton in her high school English class. She then went on to create *That Was Then, This is Now; Rumblefish* and several others that were hits. If *she* could do it, so could you!

To get started, trek over to your local library and take a peek at the current

Writer's Market. (A new one is published every year.) You'll find it in the reference section. This book will give you everything you want and more! It lists every single publisher in America. They're not all book publishers, either; some produce greeting cards, filmstrips, videos, or magazines—you name it.

Who knows? If you called a couple of your creative friends, you could probably come up with a pretty fun line of greeting cards. Watch out, Hallmark!

List a few ideas of your own:

-
-
-

WAIT! Don't say you don't have any! We've *all* got it in us! **Live up to your potential:** BE CREATIVE!

3. Get ALL the advice you can.

Just make sure when you're getting advice that you're getting it from the right people. The evidence? Sometimes their concern, occasionally their gray hair, but most often, their lifestyle. Does it reflect Jesus Christ? Are they people of integrity? If so, listen . . . and learn.

High school ISN'T life.

You're in a foreign country as you walk the halls each day. **It truly isn't the real world.** Although getting educated and prepared for life *should* rule the day, most of your classmates may think social standing, friendships, and popularity are the most important things in high school.

Trust us: High school is not the real world. But it can do the job of preparing you for life . . . if you let it.

Let's examine a few of the realities:

A. Many teachers really care about educating their students, helping teens exercise their brains, and being a good example. These are the ones from whom you should take as many classes as you can. Ask them questions. Do your assignments. Beyond this, get to know them. Since they care, they'll probably be concerned enough to give you good advice.

B. Some people cope well with life; some aren't coping well at all.

C. Many have discovered the perfect balance, while others are way out of balance. Have you noticed the people who live only for sports, or for parties, or for homework? It's not wrong to have a major focus or a single-minded goal, but **it can control you if you're not careful.**

When I (Greg) was in high school, my goal was to play pro basketball. That means I spent A LOT of time shooting hoops instead of studying. I took easy classes, didn't get too involved socially (with the right people, anyway), and basically talked myself into unreality. I was out of balance, and until I found the Lord in college, my life showed it.

If you're the perceptive type (and we hope you are), you'll see these realities right away. You'll recognize that walking the halls with between 100 and 2,500 other people about your own age is a temporary phenomenon—unique to your teenage years. Once you see the dangers of believing that this is what all of life is, you can enjoy your four high school years without letting them determine the type of person you'll be for the next fifty.

Seeking popularity with tons of the "right" kids—through parties, put-downs, or sports—just teaches you that to survive in this world you have to impress others by becoming something you're not. We've been to our high school reunions and this we know: Many, MANY of **those who lived for the crowd in high school are still living for the crowd in life.** They never learned to be themselves during those intense few years in their "high school world," so they haven't learned to adjust in the "real world."

5. PULL from Proverbs.

Proverbs is a collection of wise sayings. This one book of the Bible is **over-flowing with incredible advice** for every area of our lives. It talks about friends, wisdom, the opposite sex, being a good student, when to run and when to stay, raising your parents, how to be a good employee, gossip, cursing, being poor, and a lot of other great stuff.

There are thirty-one chapters in the book of Proverbs. Guess what? That's a chapter for every single day of the month. Try it! **We triple dare you.** It'll make a difference in your life that you won't believe.

Keep a diary of all the sayings that apply to you. And when you finish? Well, by that time it'll be a brand-new month—just in time to start all over again. *Hint:* The key here is good, solid repetition.

Not all friendships lead you in the RIGHT direction.

When I (Greg) was a junior high Campus Life director, I knew four girls who were inseparable. Not only did they call each other every day, but whenever it was time for a retreat or weekly Campus Life meetings, **you never saw one without the other three.** They were as tight as friendships could be. All four professed a faith in Christ, too. And though they were growing at different rates, you sensed that together these four could turn their school upside down for the Kingdom if they continued on the same path together.

Then . . . **high school hit.**

Kari was the pretty one of the group. No . . . gorgeous. She was the guy magnet of the four (though she had always kept things under control). But as a sophomore, she got a lot of attention from the senior guys. Soon she was dating a different football player every weekend, going to all of the parties. The other three couldn't compete. Kari was the first to abandon the group for what she thought were new and better friends.

Mindy was pretty too, but not quite as outgoing. She wanted the type of attention that Kari was getting but found it tough to break in. This fact didn't prevent her from trying, though. She didn't want to become the partyer that Kari was, but she stayed as close to her as she could just in case she could get into the same circle of "friends" Kari had.

Linda was pleasant looking, but a little heavier than the others. Left in the dust by two of her "best friends," she tried everything to get the same type of attention as Kari and Mindy. She'd attend all of the B-level parties she could find in hopes of quickly moving up, but she never quite made it into the real popular group, no matter how hard she tried.

Julie was the strongest Christian of the four and genuinely tried to be the best witness of her faith she could be. She attempted to hold the group together—and her friends' slowly maturing faith—but after just a few short months, all four were running with different friends, pursuing different paths as they tried to survive socially in that unreal world of high school. Julie kept on course, though, and still has a solid faith today. The other three are no longer making God a priority.

No one who knew these girls in junior high would have predicted that by graduation they would rarely even speak to one another.

Sure, interests change as you get older. And we're not suggesting every junior high friendship needs to be just as close in high school. This situation simply illustrates a fact: **Most of the people you are close to today may not mean a thing to you in just a few short months or years.** Sadly, people head off in separate directions, and sometimes that leads down a path away from a relationship with Jesus Christ.

What this means is . . . the people who are influencing your every decision today aren't likely to be around to see what type of person they've helped make you become. They'll have moved on to other friendships.

Are you happy with the direction in which your friends are leading you? Would you be heading this direction if you didn't have your current friends?

Friends play a huge role in shaping our future beliefs and direction in life. Every now and then, it's good to examine the road those closest to you are on, just to make sure it's a road you want to head down. Much of Planet Earth survival—

whether you're a teenager or not—is dependent on the type of friends you have.

Friends who probably won't be your friends forever.

Some bosses are JERKS.

All you want to do is make some cash, so you apply for a job at Freddy's Fabulous House of Fries. You find it fascinating how any business could actually cook a French fry 101 different ways. You interview, and to your elation, land the job of monitoring the deep-fat fryer so it stays a constant 180 degrees (one of Freddy's well-kept secrets).

You're pulling down $4.50 an hour and think you're in heaven. But the lady who's your boss on the four-to-eleven shift on Friday and Saturday nights acts like it's her mission to make you a nervous wreck. She's pulling down $5.75 as assistant manager, and her goal is to make manager so she can bring home the big bucks ($6.95 an hour). All you want to do is work your shift in peace, eat a few leftover fries (hoping your face doesn't break out any worse), and maybe get promoted to French-fry bagger (a 25¢-an-hour advancement). But for any small mistake, **she's all over you like a pit bull.**

What's her problem?

Whether it's a fast-food job today or a supervisory position on the tenth floor of the biggest bank in the state fifteen years from now, you'll always have someone you report to. This someone is usually trying to impress *her* boss. Why? **So she can move up,** make more money, move up, make more money, etc. Does she care about how she treats the people she's in charge of? Many supervisors do . . . and they'll be great to work for. But not all have good "people skills" (those actions and attitudes that communicate to the lower-level employees that they're an important part of the team). Occasionally you'll run into someone who hasn't yet *learned* how to be a leader—or they're a relational moron who shouldn't be in charge of other people!

What can you do if you're unlucky enough to get one of these types for a boss?

A. Learn how NOT to be a boss. Don't complain or argue, just take mental notes on how they treat their crew, and **try not to make the same mistakes** if you're ever in that person's shoes. (You might find *yourself* getting promoted to manager while Ms. Pit Bull is hitting the streets looking for another job!)

B. Stay friendly and try to follow orders. It's a perfect time to learn about how to respond to unreasonable authority. Why? Because from time to time you'll work for someone who doesn't know how to treat people. Count on it. If you stay and work through your feelings instead of quitting every time someone does something unfair to you (to a point, of course), **you'll develop a strong character.**

The best way to get ahead and really learn from your job is to follow orders, learn from everything you see, and let God work on your character through reasonable *and* unreasonable bosses.

Be ON time.

Emily was always late. Even though we loved being her friend, we hated her tardiness. It was a guarantee. No matter how early she tried to get ready, she was always late. Late for church, school, track meets, parties, tennis practice, youth group functions, her part-time job, and even her dates.

Finally, people began deceiving her (which wasn't right, either!). If a party started at 7:00 P.M., they told *her* to be there by 6:30. Even that didn't work! It was ridiculous. Eventually her reputation for lateness got the best of her. (She got fired from her job, and her friends stopped asking her to go places.)

Being on time just makes sense. If your boss has hired you to work the evening shift from 5:30 to 9:00 P.M., it's realistic to think he really wants you to be working at 5:30. It's also realistic to realize that if you show up at 5:45 more than twice, you probably won't have your job very long! **Employers aren't as patient as friends,** but even friends will grow weary of giving you slack.

Becoming a man or woman of integrity means keeping your word and coming through on what's expected of you. So . . . if you *say* you'll be at Taco Tim's at 6:45, *be there at 6:45*. If you're expected to be ready for your date at 8:00 P.M., don't keep him/her waiting till 8:15. **Just be on time. Enough said.**

Try NOT to be so defensive.

"Hey, Chad! Got your head in the clouds? What in the world are you day-dreaming about, man?"

"Am not. I mean, uh, nothing. I was just being observant."

"Amber, can you give me a ride to school tomorrow?"

"Again? Is that the only reason you're my friend—'cause I can drive you to school whenever you want?"

"Chris, I'm sorry you didn't make first string."

"What's it to you? I'm good at other things."

Some people are always on the defensive. They take everything so seriously—even when you're just kidding around, asking a simple favor, or trying to be friendly. They're also the ones who never learn how to take constructive criticism, and that's an important lesson to learn (unless others are criticizing the way they tie their shoes, breathe, or return lost animals to their owners).

When we're on the defensive, we're slowly hardening our hearts and minds against what *could* be helpful intervention.

Take King David, for instance. Not only did he commit adultery with Bathsheba, but he also had her husband killed so he wouldn't have to feel guilty about taking another man's wife! He had rationalized the whole thing and was feeling pretty comfortable because his defense mechanisms were in place. It doesn't take a genius to figure out that *he was in denial.* God finally got his attention through the prophet Nathan, who told him the story of a rich man with plenty of his own sheep who stole a precious lamb from a poor man. David was so angry at the man he declared he should die! Then Nathan said to him, "*You are the man!*" David was greatly ashamed and confessed his sin. (You can read the whole story in 2 Samuel 11 and 12.)

Instead of polishing your wall of defense, take time instead to remove the bricks and **really listen to what others say** when giving you constructive criticism. Who knows? You *could* be listening to a modern-day prophet!

There are REASONS for traffic laws.

Going slow in a school zone could save a child's life. Kids typically have more important things on their minds than looking both ways—like what they're going to have for a snack when they get home from school. They don't realize that a two-ton hunk of metal with four round rubber tires can actually KILL them. But you do, right?

Never assume someone sees you, has calculated your speed, and is weighing carefully the consequences of crossing the street in front of you. Also, don't think that just because a kid is riding a bike he's fully concentrating on you. He's not.

Slow down and go 20 mph in a school zone. In fact, **make it a habit** to always read the road signs ("Deaf Child Play Zone," "Deer Crossing," etc.). Traffic accidents kill over 50,000 people a year—and they're ALL accidents. People don't usually *try* to run over someone or go so fast they can't stop soon enough on the freeway. **A car can be a wonderful privilege or a lethal weapon.** It all depends on if you're paying close attention to the signs.

If you accidentally injure or kill someone, you'll carry it with you the rest of your life. The other person (and their family) will, too.

Pay attention. Obey the traffic laws, and hopefully you'll live a life free from unnecessary regret.

Learn how to put a RESUME together.

Don't wait until you're out of college and looking for your first full-time job to slap a resume together. **Start putting the pieces in place right now.**

There are all kinds of computer helps and books available to assist you in creating a one-of-a-kind, sharp resume package. And most of these materials can be purchased fairly inexpensively.

Brett was in the ninth grade when he created his first resume. The reason? His youth group was going on choir tour, and he had to earn his own money. He listed his strengths, his skills, and his experience. Then he printed them off on his home computer printer and began distributing them throughout his neighborhood.

When people within a five-block radius saw on paper that he could baby-sit, mow lawns, and do general cleanup work, it wasn't long at all before the calls began coming in, and Brett had not only earned the amount needed for choir tour, but for extra spending money as well!

What are you waiting for? Start now! (As in *right* now.) Who knows? You may become so good at it that your friends will *pay* you to create one for them!

Most people think the world revolves around THEM.

Where's the center of the universe, you ask? Just look at how people behave and the answer is obvious: around *them*.

You and us. Us and you. We simply find it incredibly difficult to do anything besides measure the state of the world by what's happening to *us*.

"Self-centered" is the word that best describes us. But if unrecognized and unchecked, **the self-centered life is the loneliest, saddest of them all.** Keeping our thoughts constantly on ourselves and our own needs leads to some very unhealthy behavior—possibly even life-threatening behavior. Consider some of these self-centered activities: overeating, smoking, drinking, drinking AND driving, taking drugs—even committing suicide! They may ALL kill you—sooner or later. When you think about it, why does anyone do these things? Maybe it's to provide a "solution" to sadness, or simply to experience some personal thrill or satisfaction. But at a terrible price to that person and to others around him!

Babies, as you'll one day find out, are the most self-centered of all God's creatures. They have no ability to do anything *besides* think of their own needs. And when their own needs aren't met, they're not bashful about letting the whole world know. What makes all of the constant care worthwhile is seeing a baby grow into a child, the child grow into a young adult, the young adult grow into a mature human being (a fifteen- to twenty-five year process!). What separates these three stages is not so much body size or a larger vocabulary, but the ability to give and to focus on others.

God would go so far as to say that **true maturity is having the heart and desire to give to others.** That means that true *immaturity* is living as if the world revolved around *you*. Like a baby.

What should you give others as you grow out of the interim stage of young adulthood?

•PATIENCE toward siblings, your parents, and your friends at school who are still struggling out of "babyhood."

•TIME to meet the needs of those around you. Large or small, you will find more joy and satisfaction by doing for others instead of waiting for them to do for you. To inconvenience yourself by missing a TV show or sharing a talent God has given you means you aren't just heading *toward* the road of maturity—you're on it. Feel good about that.

•LOVE. "By this all men will know that you are my disciples," Jesus said, "if you love one another" (John 13:35, NIV). It's the "1 Corinthians 13" type of love Jesus is talking about here. The opposite of self-centered.

The people-centered person will never lack for friends, companionship, a listening ear, and the feeling that life counts for something. That's a rare gift. But this gift awaits only those willing to admit—and act on—the belief that they ARE NOT the center of the universe.

13. You CAN make a difference.

Okay, so you've heard that phrase before. And because it's so familiar, it's easy to neglect the true meaning. How many times have you heard, "Jesus loves you!"? Or from your parents, "I love you"? After a while, we just don't recognize what those words truly mean. Both phrases, of course, mean nothing unless backed up with action. **Jesus backed up His love for us to the utmost.** Most parents have, too. They brought you into this world, put up with and nurtured you through your self-centered years (*are you still in those years?*), maybe gave up careers or career advancement, gave up time alone with each other, fed, clothed, hugged, prayed . . . and, usually, all without too much complaining.

It's easy to neglect the magnitude of words and phrases we hear all the time. To survive and thrive on Planet Earth, however, don't ever fail to recognize the power and the truth behind the statement **YOU CAN MAKE A DIFFERENCE.**

YOU . . . yes, you! The one God knit together in your mother's womb. Whom God knew before the foundation of the world. For whom Jesus Christ, the Son of God, chose to die on a cross. The one with the imperfect teeth or bad acne or spindly limbs or low GPA or shy personality. Yes, even those who seem perfect and together on the outside. YOU . . .

CAN . . . not *can't*. **You have the ability inside of you to be an agent of change today**—not tomorrow, not five years from now—to give hope or comfort to fellow human beings. To lift their head, make them smile, give them a reason for facing whatever problem may lie on their path—head on. YOU CAN . . .

MAKE . . . create something from nothing. You can see the work of your hands and the fruit of your lips—through the power of God's Holy Spirit—change the heart of a coldhearted person. You can move another soul one step closer to a real and fulfilling walk with Christ. YOU CAN MAKE . . .

A DIFFERENCE . . . sometimes, all the difference in the world. Something you say or do can fill in the "knowledge gap" a friend may have about the gospel, so that the logical next step is to invite the Lord into his life. By offering a listening ear, you can comfort a troubled heart. You can change an INDIFFERENT heart by familiar words you've heard others say your whole life.

YOU CAN MAKE A DIFFERENCE!

If life hands you lemons, you probably WON'T make lemonade. (At least not right away.)

Poster phrases are nice, cute, and often funny. Sometimes they're even true.

"When life hands you lemons, make lemonade" is one poster phrase that *isn't.*

What's a "life lemon," anyway?

•Failing a test you had to pass (and you even studied for it!).

•Grandpa or Grandma taking ill and/or dying.

•Breaking your arm before your first basketball game as a starter on varsity your senior year.

•Having a brother or sister get leukemia.

•Seeing a mom or dad walk away from the family for good.

•Getting grounded for a month for something you didn't do.

Lemons come in all shapes and sizes. You can see by the list that **some are worse than others.** When you get handed a BIG lemon, what you really want to do is throw it as far away as you can! The last thing you're thinking about is how to make something positive out of it. *Pollyanna* was a Disney movie, not real life.

The problem with "life lemons" is **you can't prevent them from coming your way.** No one can. Everyone has to handle them, usually several times in their lives.

Immediate responses to lemons range from anger to mild disappointment, with bitterness, indifference, a cold spirit, depression, and a few other emotions in between. The big question is, "Once I've put some time and distance between me and when the lemon fell in my lap, can anything good come from it? Can I make lemonade?"

Well, that's up to you. **If you want to you can;** if you don't, you won't.

We could challenge you to always make the right choice by seeing the potential good in big lemons, but that's sometimes a tall order. However, if you want to do what will help you the most in the long run, we think you're smart enough to make the best choice.

YOU don't have to even the score.

Getting back at someone who has hurt you . . . is God's business. When you take matters into *your* hands,

you're disobeying God. Sure, it may temporarily feel better to get revenge, but it

is never, as they say, sweet.

"Don't repay evil for evil. Wait for the Lord to handle the matter" (Proverbs

20:22, TLB).

Nothing more to it.

Parents grow older ... and WISER.

Losing hair, gaining weight, getting wrinkles, growing hair out of the ears— these are the telltale signs that **your parents aren't as young as they used to be.** Though their "earthsuits" are giving off signals that their youth has passed them by, their minds are still sharp (though sometimes not their memories).

Hopefully, as you've grown older, you've become a little wiser. Just living a few more years on Planet Earth has a way of giving you a significant knowledge-base from which to make good decisions. In fact, some teenagers *think* they know it all; therefore they neglect the wisdom of their parents.

Consider: If it only takes a few years for *you* to become wiser, why wouldn't the age difference between you and your parents (twenty to thirty years) give them more wisdom than you?

Most parents are deep wells of wisdom waiting to be dipped into. (No, we didn't just say your parents are dips.) So don't be a dip; go to the well.

Some things will have to be learned the HARD way.

Yeah, it's a tough lesson to learn, but **the school bus won't always wait for you** when you're running late. Policemen really *do* pull you over and issue a ticket when you speed. Courtney will eventually find out what you said about her. Your English teacher won't always let you go back to your locker to get the homework assignment you forgot to bring to class. If you don't work hard enough, you really *will* forget your lines in the school play. And eating a big lunch before a track meet will definitely make you sick.

Even though you may have already been warned about these things, there's a tendency to think, *Yeah, but it won't happen to me.* **This thinking isn't only bogus,** but it can tempt you to do your own thing in even more serious matters.

Remember when Mom said, "Don't touch that stove!" when you were two and a half? You probably went ahead and did it anyway. Was that because your mom gave you bad advice? No. She gave you *great* advice. But you, like the rest of us, wanted to be independent. You wanted to find out for yourself. It was a hard lesson, wasn't it?

Because of our own unique individuality, we often go through life saying, "Oh, yeah? How do *you* know?" And like touching a hot stove, we end up getting burned when we stray from the advice of Christian parents and God.

It's encouraging to realize that **God understands our desire to be independent**—to be "our own person." (He created us, remember?) When you get the itch to find out for yourself, try to remember that **His Word will never lead you astray.**

18 Brothers and sisters will be MORE important to you as time goes on.

Actually, they might be important right now . . . and you even act like it. Sadly, though, many teens either take their siblings for granted, or **they're in various stages of modified warfare.** Because of the competition for a quiet space, the TV, your parents' time (or money), this is understandable.

(Understandable, but not justifiable!)

Siblings can be a rich source of fun times, long talks, great memories, and later, perhaps a down payment for your first house! It's best to **work extra hard at keeping things friendly** and not let minor irritations erupt into strained relations. When your parents are growing older (or worse), they will be your only link to the past. **Treasure them.**

You **NEED** to save some money.

After you give (at minimum) your ten percent to the Lord (you *are* giving, aren't you?), the next important investment you can make is your savings account. *At least* another ten percent of whatever you receive (through a job, holiday, birthday, what you find on the pavement) should go into the bank.

Why?

Well, **there are a million reasons why,** so there isn't enough space to list them all. (Older people who have money problems might very well tell you they wish *they* had gotten into this good habit when they were younger!) **Just do it now, and you'll never regret you built this habit into your life.**

(For a bit more practical info on how to save and manage your money, see page 87.)

College will be a HUGE challenge.

Hopefully you have a few more years before you have to leave home and trek off to college—or some other place of higher learning—but you're probably already looking forward to (or dreading) that day even now.

Leaving home is tough. But it could also be the most important time of your life. The life education you'll get by going away to college is just as important as the book education. Not being around parents and siblings every day means you'll be independent. **How will you do on your own?** The answer may be determined by how well you're preparing yourself today.

•Do you fight authority at every turn? (Like teachers, bosses, and parents.) Then you'll probably be miserable. Nearly all of life is lived under the watchful eye of someone trying to make sure things are kept in order—for you and others.

•Do you like to sit around and let something electric entertain you? Then you'll waste a lot of precious time when you could be studying or working. You'll end up with bad grades and empty pockets.

•Are you a natural party animal? Then college will give you plenty of chances to experiment with drugs and alcohol. If you don't know by now what a dead end that type of life is, anything said here will be a waste of paper and ink.

•Are you developing a close relationship with God? Then you will never be alone. You'll have a best friend who promises to *always* be by your side, a constant companion with whom to talk, sharing your struggles and lonely feelings.

Whether you leave home to go to college, or into the service, or just to live and work, post high school will challenge you as you've never been challenged before. It's the last "transitional step" you'll take before you're a full-blown adult, living with all of the good and bad choices you make. **You'll have dozens of opportunities to make something of your life,** make a difference in the lives of others . . . or screw things up BIG TIME.

A little scary.

Could be fun.

Definitely . . . inevitable.

Be ready.

21 Choosing a LIFETIME love may not be easy.

It *sounds* easy. Romantic movies glamorize falling in love and getting married. Romance novels simplify finding the perfect mate. So **we tend to think it's an easy process.** Most of us think that the person with whom we fall in love is the one we'll marry. After all, isn't *love* the prerequisite for marriage?

Well, yes . . . and no.

The truth is, we can actually fall in and out of love with *several* people before we find the one with whom God wants us to spend the rest of our lives. **Just because we're in love with someone doesn't necessarily mean that's who we're supposed to marry.**

There's a much deeper issue at stake than simply being in love.

Try to see the big picture. Strive to look past the honeymoon, and instead focus on whether or not he'll be a good father or she'll be a good wife and mother. **Think about God's plan for your life.**

The real prerequisite for marriage is found in the answer to this question: Can this person and I *together* do and be more for God than I could by staying single?

If the answer is yes and you're both in love with each other, you've met the requirement for a lifetime commitment. If the answer is no, you have *no business* even *considering* marriage with this person.

Now, if you're thinking, *But if I don't marry THIS person, there may not be anyone else* . . . then **there's a deeper issue at stake,** and that's trusting God with His perfect plan for your life.

Here's a great verse to memorize and hang on to:

"But these things I plan won't happen right away. **Slowly, steadily, surely,** the time approaches when the vision will be fulfilled. If it seems slow, do not despair, for these things will surely come to pass. Just be patient! They will not be overdue a single day!" (Habakkuk 2:3, TLB).

You don't want to be a SNOB.

Though you may not consciously do anything snobbish, sometimes your actions may be interpreted that way. Not looking at people when they talk to you, not befriending anyone who believes differently than you, and harboring a grudge against someone can easily be interpreted as signs of a snob.

Remember, because you're a Christian, **people are watching your life.** So, let's do a quick nose check . . . you know, to see if yours is in the air.

ARE YOU A CHRISTIAN SNOB?

by Angela Elwell Hunt

"You can't sit with Mandi Jones!" Jessica's angry hiss stopped Traci's progress across the cafeteria.

"Why not?" Traci said, glancing over her shoulder at Jessica. "I like her. I was going to ask her to come to church with me."

"Look at that shirt she's wearing," Jessica answered. "Metallica! You can't sit with someone wearing a Metallica shirt!"

Traci looked doubtful, so Jessica hissed more loudly. "She cusses, too. What kind of a testimony is that? And **I saw her cheating in math class.** She's scum, Traci. I hate her."

Traci frowned. "I don't think she's a Christian, Jessica, so how can she act like one? And what kind of a testimony do *you* have if you hate her?"

"I don't think Christians should hang around troublemakers," Jessica answered. "We're supposed to be *different*, remember? Besides, my mom always says **you should be careful about who your friends are,** and I don't want to be friends with anyone like Mandi Jones."

Traci dutifully followed Jessica to an empty table and sat down. As they bowed their heads for a quick prayer over their food, she couldn't help wondering if being a good Christian meant ignoring people like Mandi Jones. If so, why did she feel so guilty?

ARE YOU A CHRISTIAN SNOB?

It's funny, isn't it, that something positive can become something negative? **Too much emphasis on anything can throw life out of balance,** and Christians who pride themselves on their spirituality are really projecting a very *unspiritual* attitude. Examine yourself (Psalm 139:23–24) and see if you're a "spiritual snob."

Checkpoint 1: *Are all your friends Christians?*

Once, when I was teaching twelfth graders in a Christian school, I asked how many of my students had a friend who wasn't a Christian. *Not one hand went up.*

Most of my students had gone to a Christian school since kindergarten and had practically lived at church. They didn't have time for Little League or Girl Scouts or hanging out in the neighborhood, and by the twelfth grade, they didn't even *know* anyone who didn't claim to be a Christian.

But wasn't it wonderful to be in an all-Christian environment? you might ask. Well, yes and no. At times it felt like we were all sitting in an algae-covered, stagnant pond. You see, water has to have an outlet to keep moving, and my Christian school students weren't moving at all. They were in a spiritual rut about six feet deep. **They weren't dead and buried, but they might as well have been.**

"You are the light of the world," Jesus told us. People don't hide lamps under baskets; they hold them up high so the light can shine out to the world. YOU are the light of *your* world! God has placed you where you are for a purpose. **Find a way and a place to shine.**

Checkpoint 2: *Do you look down on others who are less spiritual than you are?*

Jessica didn't want to be seen with Mandi Jones because Mandi was wearing a Metallica T-shirt. But Mandi didn't claim to be a Christian.

Think about it: **Why do we Christians get upset when unsaved people act like unsaved people?** We become new creatures only when we accept Jesus, right? So, we can't blame someone for not walking and talking like a Christian if she isn't one. When Jesus met Zacchaeus, a cheating tax collector, He didn't shun or scold him. Instead, He *honored* Zacchaeus by choosing his house for dinner. Zacchaeus became a new man after that day.

When Jesus met the woman who had been caught red-handed in adultery, He didn't faint or yell or have a fit. Instead, the Savior simply waited for the angry crowd to leave, then He told the woman to go and sin no more.

Would Jesus have left Mandi, the Metallica fan, to eat lunch by herself? I don't think so.

But, you say, *my parents would have a fit if I started hanging around the wild kids at school!* You're probably right. And **if you have parents who care about your choice of friends, you're lucky.**

But everything depends on how you define "hanging around." It's one thing to have a girl like Mandi as your best buddy, and it's another thing to be nice and say "hi" to her in the halls.

Our closest friends influence us the most. While

your parents probably don't want you spending time with someone whose ideas and goals are completely opposite from yours, they won't mind if you're nice to Mandi and invite her to church with you.

Checkpoint 3: *Do you forgive your Christian friends for their mistakes?*

Though the Bible tells us not to judge, it's very easy to turn up our spiritual noses at mistakes other Christians make. Sometimes we can forgive an unbeliever for cursing or cheating, but if a *Christian* falls into the same temptation, whoa! Snub city!

But, like the bumper sticker says, *Christians aren't perfect, just forgiven.* So strive to forgive your Christian friends (seventy times seven like the Bible says) and remember that you'll make mistakes, too. We're *all* in the process of learning and growing. **Since God forgives us, we need to forgive others.**

Summing It Up

Jesus didn't spend all His time with the disciples but went wherever people would receive Him. Though He was the only sinless man who ever lived, He didn't think himself too "holy" to eat with sinners. He spent time with lost people who needed Him. And though His disciples continually argued, misunderstood Him, and ran away when the going got tough, Jesus continued to love and forgive them.

Take stock of your spiritual life this week. **If you don't know anyone who isn't a Christian, walk down your street and make a new friend.** Accept people the way Jesus did, without judgment or condemnation. And if any of your Christian friends mess up, write them an encouraging note and tell them you'll be praying for them. Most important, ask them to pray for *you*.

This article by Angela Elwell Hunt first appeared in the April 1994 issue of Brio *magazine.*

FRIENDSHIPS

Which kind of friend should you be? Close? Casual? Really, really tight? Well, it depends on whom you're befriending. Yes, **Jesus told us to reach out to everyone** . . . but there's a big difference between reaching out to someone (like having lunch with Mandi) and becoming *intimate*.

Friendships naturally fall into four different levels.

Level One: *Acquaintances*. Everyone you know well enough to say "hi" to falls into this category—the man next door, the guy whose locker is down the hall, the teacher you had last year. I believe that God brings every one of these people into your life for a purpose.

Level Two: *Casual*. Casual pals share your interests. You talk together easily because you have a few things in common.

Level Three: *Close*. These friends usually have similar backgrounds and share life goals. Close friends are a strong influence on each other.

Level Four: *Intimate*. Your deepest friendships are found here. **Intimate friends have the freedom to correct each other honestly.** They are also committed to one another through good and bad.

You'll have many friendships throughout your life on all of these levels. Jesus cared about everyone He met, yet His *disciples* were His close friends (they shared some similar values). Peter, James, and John were closer still, and the Bible tells us that John was probably Jesus' best earthly friend.

Bottom line? **Strive to be Jesus to your world.** Be courteous to EVERYONE. But be selective when you pair up. Close and intimate friends will mold and influence you . . . so choose those friendships wisely.

Learn to say NO.

Yeah, we know, **sometimes the pressure to do something is incredibly tempting.**

Like punching a hole in your tent so you can still see the stars when you're camping out. Or tying your little brother onto the back of your bicycle when he's being annoying and dragging him around the block a few times. Or cutting off the tops of all your shoes so you never have to remove them, or getting new ones and working really hard to get them scuffed up just right so they won't *look* new.

We're kidding. **We know you'd never do any of those kinds of things.** But what about *other* kinds of temptations? Like not giving back the extra change you received from the clerk who's new and didn't count right? Or knowing that your curfew is midnight, you slip in at 12:30, and the next morning when your dad says, "Did you make curfew?" you answer, "Are you kidding? I know how important that is! Think I'd even *consider* missing it?"

When you're tempted to do that stuff, it's important that you say NO! to the temptation. Do you know why? Because **Jesus Christ never buckled under pressure.** And since *He* didn't, **He expects the same of you.** The cool thing is He knows it takes a lot of strength to say no to temptations. That's why **He'll let you lean on Him** and use *His* strength instead of your own to overcome any and *all* pressure-filled moments.

Older people are USUALLY wiser.

Have you ever known people who have all the answers? They're probably the type you don't want to talk to or hang around with. So if you come in contact with an older adult who acts like (or says) he or she knows all the answers, be wary.

But older folks DO have a few things going for them you don't:

A. They have lived more days on Earth, so they probably have been through more experiences than you (thus, knowing what to do and what not to do when a situation comes up).

B. They have made more mistakes than you have (and have hopefully learned a few things from them).

C. **They can see the "big picture" a little better than you.** That is, they know what things to sweat and what things to let roll off their back. (Most things, they'll probably say, aren't that important to sweat.)

D. They've experienced more of God's grace and probably have a pretty good handle on what He's like.

E. Believe it or not, they had most of the same feelings about the opposite sex that you have (or will have) and were challenged in a similar way.

There are others, but you get the picture. Not all older folks can give good advice, but whenever you see gray hair, there's usually a well inside that runs deep. There's gold in their years (and their mouth, too, probably) that needs to be mined . . . there's wisdom—more wisdom than you have yet. Because of that you have a choice: **Tap in to it, or be the type who**

learns the hard way.

Our advice is to **be a question-asker as often as possible.** Just because you ask questions doesn't mean you have to follow every answer you get. It only means **you'll have a few more options.**

But older people are not always SMARTER.

We've said older people are wiser,

but that doesn't make them perfect . . . or smarter. Some are so used to simple ways that they don't understand how complicated it is to live in the age of information. Technology has made our world a little different than theirs. They know a lot, **but they don't know everything.**

26 { When you're wrong ... ADMIT it!

Everyone blows it, including you. The

Bible is packed full of people who blew it. Remember the apostle Peter? He was the one to whom Jesus said, "You're rock-solid, just like a huge stone! I can build my church on someone like you!"

And we tend to think, *Yeah, Peter was quite a guy! He walked on water, got to go to the Mount of Transfiguration with Jesus and meet a couple of saints from the past, healed a lame man, and prayed over a dead girl until she started breathing again! Yeah, he was quite a guy!*

But he was also the guy who boldly told Jesus at the Last Supper that he'd never forsake Him, then **just a few hours later** blatantly denied that he even *knew* Jesus. And he didn't blow it just once. He denied His Master *three times!*

Judas sure blew it, too, didn't he? Jesus had barely finished washing Judas' feet and calling him "friend," when he planted the kiss of betrayal on His Master's face.

Two disciples. Both in the close company of Jesus Christ for three solid years. Both heard the same sermons, saw the same miracles, enthusiastically proclaimed the same Kingdom message. But both denied Jesus.

Only one, though, had the humility to admit he was wrong. **Peter was just as guilty as Judas.** Maybe even more! Judas denied Christ only once, and Peter denied Him three times. Yet, Peter was not so full of pride that he couldn't humble himself before His Lord.

Jesus forgave Peter. He *would* have forgiven Judas, too, if only he'd asked. A humble, contrite heart goes a loooong way with our heavenly Father.

We're all guilty, aren't we? All of us disappoint our Master. **We all blow it.** Yet when we come to Christ with a repentant heart and genuinely seek His forgiveness, we are cleansed.

Humility will go a long way in other areas of life, too. You said something about Eric that you shouldn't have, and now he's found out about it. Instead of coming up with a million excuses to justify yourself, simply go to him and **admit you were wrong.**

"Hey, Eric. I was way outta line, man. It's my fault. I'm really sorry. Can you forgive me? I want things to be cool between us."

The sooner you learn the act of humility the better your life will be. It's a lesson you'll use the rest of your life, not just while you're in high school, youth group, and college. It can even save your job or earn you a promotion in the work world.

Why?

Because **everyone admires someone who can admit their faults,** take the blame, and make it right.

Humility.

We don't hear much about it anymore. Learn to make it part of *your* vocabulary.

27. Your vote COUNTS.

When you hit age eighteen, you'll face decisions a couple of Tuesdays a year. **Should I vote? Or should I stay home and watch TV?**

Since voting is a primary way you can make a statement about your views on a wide range of important issues, we strongly suggest, adamantly implore, with conviction and enthusiasm, with unbridled emotion, with a look of resolve in our eyes . . . asking you very nicely (using "please" and "thank you")—VOTE! And not just vote in presidential years, but on all the local stuff, too. VOTE! **You may not think it counts, but it does.** VOTE!

Probably the most important reason you should vote is you can't EVER complain about ANYTHING the city, county, state, or federal government does unless you've voted. But if you have walked into that little voting booth and used that pointer thing to stick into the hard paper, or pulled down the levers, or completed the broken arrow (or whatever method your precinct uses), *then* **you can complain all you want!** And that's a good feeling.

You'll reap EXACTLY what you sow.

It's true: **Whatever you dish out will eventually come back at you.** The apostle Paul punches us between the eyes with this truth in Galatians 6:7b: "A man reaps what he sows" (NIV).

When I (Susie) was a youth minister, there was a girl in our youth group who didn't have many close friends. But she was incredibly kind. She sent little notes and cards to other kids in the group every single week.

Guess what happened when she had to go to the hospital? Teens from our group rallied around her with prayer, visits, kindness, and lots of attention. She had generously sowed many seeds of love and outreach, and they sprouted and came back to her in full bloom.

Dale was a guy who always got what he wanted. He was a slick talker, and people were often swept away by his slickness. But Dale was manipulative. He didn't mind using people to get what he wanted. If he had to step on someone to get ahead, he thought nothing of it. **Their loss was his gain.** If someone ever disagreed with him, he made a careful mental note and spent weeks creating ways to embarrass that person. There was a saying about Dale: "He'll never forgive you for a wrong he has done you."

In other words, people eventually began to see through him, and they didn't like what they saw. They realized he held grudges, only had *his* interests at heart, and even compromised his values.

Though at one time he was surrounded by lots of support and tons of friends, today he's a lonely young man. You guessed it, he's reaping exactly what he sowed.

Do you want a happy life? Do you want to be someone your friends can trust? Then **sow the seeds** *right now!*

LEARN to forgive.

Forgiving those who have hurt you is probably the toughest thing you'll ever have to learn. If it's so hard, why do you need to learn it? Because **unforgiveness creates an angry and bitter heart.** And anger, after it's settled way down deep inside you, is kind of like a rotten egg. Not only does it smell bad, but it turns color. And the color of rotten, bitter, angry unforgiveness is depression. It's true! Depression is often anger turned inward, and **it can kill you emotionally.**

I (Susie) met MaWee in Chiang Mai, Thailand. She's a beautiful, bright fifteen-year-old girl whose life has spelled *n-i-g-h-t-m-a-r-e* for most of her childhood.

She was born in Burma (now called Myanmar, a country in southeast Asia, close to Thailand). When she was six, her mom died. When she was ten, her opium-addicted stepdad sold her for $100 to a Chinese woman who wandered into their village recruiting young preteens for prostitution.

MaWee was taken from her small village to Bangkok, Thailand. Not only was it a different country, but the cultures and customs were also different. Even the language was foreign. You can imagine how frightened she was!

She was taken to a brothel, a place where prostitutes work. The owner began selling her to various men in the city for nights of evil pleasure.

Eventually the police raided the place and took MaWee to a children's shelter, where she scrubbed and mopped floors for three years. From there she was sent to the city of Chiang Mai (about twelve hours from Bangkok) to the New

Life Center, a ministry outreach to prostitutes.

The assistant housing mother began reading the Bible to MaWee and telling her about God's great love. MaWee had never heard anything like this before! **She was mesmerized** by this Jesus of the Bible.

She began going to church and eventually gave her life to Christ. Though she's only in the ninth grade right now, I asked her what she wanted to do with her life. "I want to continue schooling," she said, "so I can go to Bible College and become an evangelist. I want to tell everyone about Jesus Christ and His great love."

I looked in her big gray eyes and said, "MaWee, are you angry? I mean, so many bad things have happened to you. Aren't you a little bitter?"

She smiled . . . an electric smile that reached from ear to ear. Her eyes twinkled as she said, "Oh no! God forgives me; therefore, I forgive the people who hurt me. I'm not angry anymore. Jesus has taken my anger away. I just want to tell others about Him."

Wow!

Maybe your life hasn't been that rough, but **you've probably been hurt pretty badly by people you love.** Instead of harboring a grudge, can you let it go? **Jesus died for your hurt.** Instead of hanging on to it, **can you give it to Him?** If you don't, it will eventually destroy you.

Go ahead.

Let it go.

Give it up.

Turn it over.

Forgive!

Be committed to good things, but don't get

OVER-COMMITTED.

Do you want to learn to get the most out of life? Do you want to be able to do a few things YOU want to do, as opposed to things others are asking you to do? Do you want to have enough time to spend with the Lord each day? **The Bible talks about** guarding your heart, but along with that, we've discovered that if you don't *guard your time*, it will get stolen. You may wind up doing a lot of good things, but good things aren't always the right things. Over-commitment is a disease that, unless checked early, will carry on into adulthood. Too-busy adults are not happy adults.

It's okay to say no to opportunities that come your way. Whether it's playing on a church league softball team, being on a committee at school, or volunteering at the local mission, **it's okay to be selective.** We're not saying don't get involved with anything. You should be committed to serving others *and* taking time for yourself.

Satan will rob our joy of living in two ways: lack of involvement and over-involvement.

Lack of involvement promotes a selfish, sometimes lazy attitude that only looks out for personal comfort. "Couch potato" is a good word picture. Over-involvement is often a way to mask insecurities. The reasoning goes, "If I can stay real busy, I won't have time to think about my (perceived) failures, or confront weaknesses that should be turned into strengths."

How do you know when you're too committed or not committed enough? Well, often you won't, unless you find good friends who will be objective enough to tell you the truth. **Every Christian needs someone to confide in** about how we're investing our time. Without a friend to ask us the tough questions, we'll naturally gravitate toward over—or under—involvement. This is called being "accountable" to another person. **Do it.**

Enjoy something EVERY day.

And we don't mean TV, your best CD, or that new *Brio* or *Breakaway* that came in the mail. We're thinking more along the lines of God's creation.

·People. A conversation with Mom, Dad, Grandma, Grandpa, a little child . . . even your brother or sister! People can be a pain, but **most of the time, people are amazing.** They can make you smile, think, and appreciate life to a greater degree.

·Nature. A sunset, rainbow, clouds, wind, snow, rain, ocean, river, stream, mountains, desert, flowers, insects, seashells, trees, birds, dogs, and cats. When you think about it, there's a ton of stuff to be amazed at—stuff you'd normally take for granted because you see it every day.

We promise: If you become the type of person who can **enjoy something about God's creation each new day,** you will truly have a happy life. By keeping wonder and amazement more on your mind than pessimism and problems, you will be a rich person—not in money, perhaps, but in joy. Others will want to hang out with you . . . and *you'll* want to hang out with you! You'll like being you because each day you'll have new discoveries and new small joys to look forward to.

Here's the challenge: For one week, make a "Creation" journal. Take it with you and **write down what you notice or something you do that is kind of amazing.** At first, you may be writing down things that seem normal, but when you look at them a second time . . . they're actually AMAZING! You can try this on vacation, Christmas or spring break, summer, or even while you're in school.

One week . . . . **Please.**

Don't let anything or anyone CONTROL you.

It's incredible what people let control them. You've heard about people who are addicted to alcohol and drugs, but here's a list of other things that can control someone:

- •TV
- **.Music**
- •Fashion; looking just right to impress others
- **.A boyfriend or girlfriend**
- •Studies, homework, learning (believe it or not)
- •Food
- •Staying skinny
- •Sex; pornography; flirting
- •Weightlifting; attaining the perfect physique
- **.Sports; or a particular sport**
- •Hobbies
- •Making money

We won't say the list is endless, but when people get out of balance or don't have anyone to hold them accountable on how they're spending their time (or money, or thought-life), it's easy to get OVERLY INTO something. What starts as something harmless (sometimes) winds up controlling **most of their waking moments.**

As you will notice by this list, some of these potential "addictions" are socially and/or biblically acceptable. There isn't a commandment that says, "Thou shalt not work extra hard at keeping your weight down." But we have known girls (and some guys) so obsessed with having 0% body fat, they either don't eat (*anorexia nervosa* is the medical term), or they "binge and purge," eat and throw up (*bulimia*). They're addicted to being "skinny." For some, **this addiction is deadly.**

The apostle Paul said, "I won't be mastered by anything."

You're young. For some reading these pages, you haven't had enough years to form an unhealthy addiction. But **bad habits learned early are tough to break**—*tough*, not impossible.

Whether you think you're addicted to something or not, talk to a parent, friend, or youth leader, and just ask that person to give you an honest response to this question: "Do you think I'm overdoing it in any area of my life? **Am I addicted to something without even knowing it?"**

If you're afraid to ask someone that question, the chances are that you ARE either addicted or on the verge of being addicted to something or someone. The longer you keep silent, the tougher it will be to pull yourself out of it. We humans—Christians or not—are pretty good at hiding our inadequacies and "secret sins." We feel that if someone knows about them, they won't like us anymore, so we stay quiet. Most of the time, however, the exact opposite is true. **Admitting failure is a sure sign of maturity, and people are drawn to those who face themselves in an honest and open way.**

Do you value honest and transparent people? Hopefully you do. **Seek to become what you value most.**

Your HORMONES can make you moody.

If you're between the ages of eleven and seventeen, you're probably going through something called puberty. Yeah, **we know, you've heard all of this before.** That's why we'll keep this short.

For about two years your body will be going through all sorts of changes. That means **the chemicals God has placed inside you are going berserk.** They've got a job to do getting you ready for adulthood.

While everyone responds differently, you'll probably sleep more, eat more, grow more and . . . be more moody. You could even fly off the handle over practically nothing, and then scratch your head wondering where that came from (along with your parents).

This is the perfect time to practice your apology skills. You can't blame poor behavior on hormones and expect everyone to understand. So when you yell at your little brother at the top of your lungs because he borrowed one of your tapes, you've overreacted. Apologize and make things right. While the hormones may encourage you to do strange stuff, you're still responsible. Take care of it, and move on.

Someone YOU know has been sexually abused.

The statistics are high: **One out of every four girls and one out of every ten boys will be sexually abused by a family member.** And that's of reported cases only!

There are several other kinds of sexual abuse besides incest (sexual abuse within the family). So with numbers that high, it's likely that at least one person in your youth group and in each of your classes at school has been sexually abused.

Never joke about it.

Ever.

And **if you think someone you know is being abused, don't be silent.** Go to a guidance counselor and **get some help.**

Some parents feel STUCK in their jobs.

Like most people when they were young, **your parents felt they could set the world on fire,** that someday they could make a difference. Perhaps they went off to college. Then they got married and started to make a life for their family. When kids (YOU) came along, an even higher calling rang in their heads: "We have to make sure we can make enough money to feed, clothe, and save for braces and college! This is the real world!"

In your family maybe **both your parents hold down jobs to make ends meet;** or maybe your dad goes to work while your mom stays home to take care of you and your siblings. Or maybe you live with your mom and she has to support the family all on her own. Whatever the particulars, many parents find ways to work this all out without too many extra worries. But some, probably even more than we realize, are stuck. They've abandoned their dreams of having their lives make a difference in the world to make sure the mortgage is paid, and there's gas in the car and food on the table. Consequently they've had to take and/or stay in jobs that perhaps won't lead them very far. Such jobs pay the bills, but for eight to ten hours a day **they cope with a life quite different from their dreams.** Not that they would complain about their lot (especially to their kids), but they do occasionally feel that life is passing them by.

One or both of your parents may be people who feel "stuck." And now, since you're a teenager, they have the added knowledge that it's important to you to stay with your friends until graduation. Moving to a different city for a better job would not necessarily be the best thing to do . . . for you. So they stay in their jobs for another four to eight years until their lives are separated from yours. By this time, they're probably too old to make any changes that will help recapture that feeling of making a difference in the world.

All of this could seem very depressing, but that's not our goal in bringing this up. We know, and most Christian parents know, that God is involved, too. It's not the kids' fault that Dad or Mom stay in jobs they feel stuck in. **Even parents must learn what contentment is about.** And they need to establish long-term relationships with co-workers and neighbors to help lead them to Christ, and they can't do that if they're moving around every two years. So it's not always bad they stay in one town or at one job for a long time.

It's just tough to handle sometimes.

So the next time you think about it, ask your dad or mom some deep questions:

- "Are you happy in your work?"

- "Do you feel like you're making a difference?"

- "What were your lifetime goals when you were in your early twenties?"

- "Now that I'm here taking up space and eating your food and borrowing your money, do you ever feel stuck?"

Then, no matter what their answers are, say something like, "I don't know all of the feelings you're going through, but I appreciate the sacrifices you're making for the family. I'm having some pretty good growing-up years, and a lot of the reason is because you're so dedicated to providing for all of us. I appreciate you."

If you wanted to go the second mile, of course, you could continue your statement by saying something like, "And if you feel you need to change jobs or move to another city to better provide for the family or do something you'll enjoy more, I'm open to talking about it with the rest of the family."

Again, this advice won't relate to *every* teen reading this book, but it will for *some*. **Parents who feel stuck need an extra dose of love and encouragement to know that their lives really are making a difference.** Perhaps it's not earth-shaking, but it's helping you grow up to be a mature person—so it IS making a difference.

Not every job you have will be "fulfilling," but it will HELP you get where you're going.

You say it's not your lifetime goal to master the question, "Would you like fries with your burger?" Good. But you have to start somewhere.

You might be lucky enough to find a first job you love—doing something related to your life goals. It may be an entry-level position, but you'll be able to see that it's a step on the way. It's more likely, though, that **your first job will seem to have nothing at all to do with your goals.** You'll probably have between five and fifteen jobs that you're not all that crazy about before you finally hit on the one you're really going to love. But while you're making hamburgers, sweeping floors, waiting tables, or sacking groceries, **you are gaining real-life job skills** that will serve you well in the future (besides making some money!). You're "paying your dues," gaining experience, and learning your way so **you'll be ready for that dream job of the future.**

I (Greg) never worked in a fast-food restaurant, but I did work five summers in a bean cannery during high school and college. I also worked on a farm, repairing fences and shoveling cow . . . stuff. I chopped wood for eight hours a day, answered phones in a college psychology department, did yard work for rich people, and a bunch of other little jobs that had nothing to do with my lifetime ambitions.

I "paid my dues" before I finally got to do what I wanted to do—help young people. Along the way I got through college, paid my bills, learned a few things that have helped me in life, made some friendships that have lasted, and been used by God to move pre-Christians closer to a relationship with Jesus Christ. At the time, I didn't view these jobs as all that "fulfilling"; they were just a means to an end.

It's OK to have jobs that aren't the final destination.

Part of the highway that *leads* to the destination both you and the Lord want you to reach is working hard at menial jobs. So pay your dues and *learn* from everything you do to make a buck.

REAL friends will tell you the truth.

How can you tell when you've got real friends?

They'll let you know when . . .

. . . you need a breath mint (without letting everyone within earshot know your breath could kill a sewer rat).

. . . they can help you with homework and tell you when you should work on it by yourself.

. . . you hurt someone else with your words.

. . . you hurt them with your words.

. . . you're hurting yourself by doing stupid things.

. . . you're wrong.

. . . you're right.

. . . they can listen to your problems, and when it's not a good time to listen because they're preoccupied.

Real friends are rare because of the type of honesty required. When you find one, do all you can to keep him/her. An honest friend who only has your welfare in mind is worth more than a hundred who'll tell you what they think you *want* to hear.

It's been said that at the end of your life if you can count five close friendships, you'll be a rich person. An honest friend will most likely end up on that list. We know you're not used to assessing the value of something based on what you have at the end of your life, but in this case—try. And by the way, **are you that type of friend to anyone?**

PEOPLE are what God's most concerned with.

There are only two eternal things in this world: God's Word and the souls of people. Everything, EVERYTHING else is temporary. It won't make it to heaven.

God wants us to pursue Him through His Word, but **He also wants us to be involved with people.** Remember . . .

Jesus died for people.

Jesus prayed for people (see John 17).

Jesus cried over people. He healed people. He showed compassion for people. Good people, bad people . . . it didn't matter. Eternity and the unseen world were as real to Jesus as today and the seen world is to us. That's why **His whole life was invested in freeing people** from the bondage of sin and showing them the free gift of salvation they could have in Him.

There will be good people in your life that you'll love spending time with, people who are easy to talk to, people who won't lead you in the wrong direction.

Then there will be difficult people—those you don't click with, and those you just don't like. You don't have anything in common with them, and they're not too interested in spending time with you.

To Jesus, difficult people are just as high a priority as good or easy ones. Why? He sees the big picture; He sees eternity, both heaven and hell. He knows heaven is too wonderful to be missed and hell is too awful to be endured. He's in touch with these two realities . . . and He wants us to be in touch with them, too.

A speaker once said that "our hearts should break at the same things that break the heart of Jesus."

A lost soul breaks the heart of Jesus. When you see people shaking their fist at God through their actions or attitudes, fight the urge to sneer or turn away. They're breaking God's heart. And if they don't break our hearts, it's likely we're not in touch with God's heart.

You'll have many priorities to pursue here on Planet Earth—money, marriage, a career, sports, enjoyment, perhaps children—**but few are as important as people.**

You can't conjure up a heart for people. God must give it to you. If you understand the importance of seeing people the way God sees them, make a commitment each day to pray a simple prayer: *This day, Lord, give me the heart for people that you have. What breaks your heart today, let it break mine.*

If you do that, **God will use you to bring others to Him** more than you could ever imagine.

Sooner or later other people's BAD choices will affect you negatively.

I'll never forget the day my dad took my brother, sister, and me (Greg) on a drive out to the lake. His objective was to tell us he was leaving our mom. He did it while he drove so he wouldn't have to look us in the eye. At twelve, I didn't know what to think besides, *This really stinks.* So I got to go through adolescence without a dad around at a time I needed him most.

His poor choice affected me negatively. **I didn't do anything to deserve it,** but I had to face the consequences.

A student in my Campus Life group was taking his niece around trick-or-treating on Halloween many years ago. Five minutes after they stopped by my house, a friend came running to my door. "Jason's just been hit by a car." I ran a block to the scene **just as the paramedics were arriving.** I drove to the hospital and listened with stunned silence as the ER physician told the family their son was dead. A drunk driver had cut short the life of a nice kid. That driver's poor choices robbed Jason of his life, as well as his parents of seeing him grow up, marry, and perhaps give them grandchildren to spoil.

Are you getting the picture? Poor choices from others will affect you in a bad way. **Count on it.** A relative, friend, or stranger will do something—purposely or by accident—that will cause you pain or grief.

How will you respond?

That remains to be seen, of course. You can get really mad, hold a grudge, and harbor bitter feelings for years, thus letting that one poor choice by someone else have control over you. Or you can realize that **God offers no promise that you won't ever have to pay the consequences** of someone else's mistakes—except the one Jesus gave: "In this world you will have trouble. But take heart! I have overcome the world" (John 16:33b, NIV).

God can make sense out of anything that seems senseless (Romans 8:28). It may take a few years to learn the lessons, or you may never understand the "Why?" of it while on this earth. But do all you can to let the anger or bitterness pass you by. Your emotional survival on Planet Earth may depend on it.

Happiness is the WRONG goal to shoot for.

Not once in the Bible does it say to make it your goal to be happy. It talks about being at peace with all men (Romans 12:18), to live contented with what you have (Philippians 4:12), to love each other (John 13:34–35), and tons of other choice, practical, and attainable goals, but never does it mention happiness. That's an American goal. (You remember, "Life, liberty and the pursuit of happiness.")

Being happy is good. Okay, *very* good. And **when we're happy, we should thank God for it.** But constant happiness—as we're sure you've discovered—doesn't occur! So pursuing things or circumstances that will just make you happy will lead to major disappointments. It's a goal and expectation that can't be orchestrated. You can't push buttons to make it happen.

Happiness occurs along the way. It's often unexpected. In fact, the more you try to manufacture happiness, the less happy you'll be. The older you get, the more you'll realize there are a few higher goals to pursue anyway. God's peace that passes all understanding is perhaps the main one. **If you can learn the secret of living at peace with God, with others, and with yourself, you'll find more happiness than you can imagine.** Promise.

41 } Don't let OTHERS determine your self-worth.

Base your sense of security in God and God alone. After all, HE thinks you're so special, He even calls you by name. Check it out:

"I have called you by name; you are mine" (Isaiah 43:1b, TLB).

"And I will give you treasures hidden in the darkness, secret riches; and you will know that I am doing this—I, the Lord, the God of Israel, the one who calls you by your name" (Isaiah 45:3, TLB).

"I called you by name when you didn't know me" (Isaiah 45:4b, TLB).

You are so special to God that He even knows the number of hairs on your head! He cares about everything that concerns you. Shouldn't that make you feel pretty good about yourself? Imagine! **The Creator of the universe cares about YOU!** He cares about that test you're not ready for in science class. He cares that Josh is saying unkind things about you. **Since God cares so much about you, you're pretty valuable.**

So when others make fun of you, when you blow the history quiz, when you don't make the team, and when Jamie doesn't even know you exist, don't start thinking, *I'm worthless.*

You're NOT worthless. You're more valuable to God than precious jewels. **He's crazy in love with you.** In fact, He loves you as if you were the only person in all the world to love!

Now THAT should make you feel pretty good about yourself. And THAT'S what determines your self-worth. It's all in the hands of your Father.

Don't go OVERBOARD on sleep.

Yeah. Yeah. Yeah. You're a growing teen, and your body is changing, and you need lots of sleep so your cells can replenish themselves. We know. We said the same thing when *we* were high school sophomores.

Sleep is good. We all need it. But **you can overdo a good thing.** Strive NOT to be one of those people who always oversleeps. **Sleeping more than you need can just be laziness.** And we don't want you making a habit of *that!*

Besides, if you're in the habit of oversleeping, you miss out on a section of life that you can never relive. Think about it: TIME is the most valuable commodity you own. Once you use it up, you can't *ever* call it back. So be extremely careful about how you spend your time. **When you oversleep, you're wasting time.**

Even GOD has something to say about sleeping: "If you love sleep, you will end in poverty. Stay awake, work hard, and there will be plenty to eat!" (Proverbs 20:13, TLB).

Try this: Set your alarm five minutes earlier tomorrow and **get a head start on your day.**

Some homeless people want help; others don't, but it's a good idea to try to do SOMETHING.

I (Greg) was heading to my hotel in downtown Denver a while back when I was approached by a man—a man with a definite slur and a slight smell of booze.

"Got any spare change, mister?" he said. "I haven't eaten all day."

I had spare change, but I've made it my habit to **never give it out.** Instead, I took the guy over to a pizza place and paid $1.75 for a big slice of pizza and a water. He tried to tell me his story, but I've heard so many of them, **I had no way of knowing** whether it was true or not. I walked out with the man, and a stranger who saw me go in with him said, "Bless you, sir. That was good."

I smiled weakly as I headed back to my cozy, expensive room.

What did I really do? I thought. *Did I help him or prolong his pain? Well, at least he didn't take my money for liquor.*

I *think* I did the right thing, but whenever I come in contact with a homeless person, **I never feel I've done enough.** The guy needed more than I could give him . . . far more! Yet perhaps it was enough. It proved to be a great reminder for me that from those who have been given much, much is required. Pizza at that moment was far better than a spare quarter.

If you live in a big town or a small city, you've probably seen them. They're walking the streets, sleeping in parks, panhandling for spare change, and generally doing what they've learned to do to survive.

A high percentage are mentally impaired in some way but are ineligible to be cared for in state mental health hospitals. It's not possible for some of these people to hold down a job. So they roam the streets. Sometimes for years . . . even decades.

Others are families just way down on their luck. They were living from paycheck to paycheck anyway when unemployment hit and they couldn't make the rent. Before they knew what to do about it, **they were looking for cars to sleep in.** Many have let drugs and alcohol ruin their ability to be functioning human beings; many are young people who have run away from a bad home situation. Whatever the reasons that people become homeless (and there are many!), once they're living on the streets, it becomes extremely difficult for them to get a job. How many employers are willing to take a chance on someone who doesn't even have an address? (You can't even receive welfare without an address.)

The tendency is to ignore these people as part of the scenery or silently ridicule them for being what they are. Neither are good options. So **what should you do?** Empty your pockets of change every time someone asks? Bad move. You'll get them away from you, but you may not be helping them do anything more than buy their next bottle of Thunderbird.

Doing what I did, taking them someplace to get food, involves a little more time, money, and dare (especially if you're a female), but it's often the best you can offer. **Listening to their story is good for you — and them.** After I listen, a bigger question always hits me whenever I leave the presence of a street person: What would Jesus do?

He'd feed street people, clothe them, help train them or find them work, love them over the long haul . . . and show them the Father's character by His actions. He'd talk to them about God too, if He felt the time was right.

That's what thousands of people are doing each day on city streets throughout the country (and the world). They're going where Jesus would go, doing what Jesus would do, because our Lord died for the homeless as much as He died for the rich. Anytime you see a person in need, Jesus wants to be there.

Does He want to be there through you?

Maybe so. If you've been praying about what to do with your life, helping the homeless (or others in need) is a great way to invest your heart and the gifts God has given you. **Start small at first** to see if you're cut out for this type of ministry (not everyone is). Volunteer at your local mission or street ministry for a few days. If nothing else, **it will open your eyes** to the fact that these are real people in desperate need of emotional, physical, and spiritual help.

You'll need a **TON** of patience every day.

Most people have it within them to be absolute airheads. Parents, teachers, friends, total strangers—**they're all in need of a brain transplant** every now and then. They say and do dumb stuff that will either tick you off, hurt your feelings, or make you go away scratching your head and wondering what planet they came from.

Why do they do dumb things that try your patience? The same reason you do it to them! You're a human-type sinful person whose "job" it is to pass through life making mistakes. While you won't be able to ignore everything people do or say to you, just being able to predict that they'll occasionally push you to your limit should give you the strength to cut them some slack.

You've heard it said, "Patience is a virtue." Well, whoever said that is right. Make it a virtue you want to incorporate into your life.

P.S. By all means **pray for patience** (how else are you ever going to get any?), but BEWARE: God *will* test your patience by allowing even more brain-dead people to do dumb stuff to you. And even if you don't pray for patience, you'll still get plenty of chances to practice. **God wants you to learn patience whether you want to or not!**

Cars BREAK down.

Talk about a patience-tester! This is probably the reason why God even allowed the automobile to be invented. *Hmmm, God wonders, what can I allow my creation to invent that will benefit them most of the time, but cause them to realize they're not so smart after all?*

The car.

You can kick and scream, yell and swear, but that won't help anything if you have to pull your car over or if you have to soak hundreds of dollars into it for repairs. Your only defense against cars breaking down is to (1) realize it's going to happen, usually at the worst possible time, and (2) learn a few things about cars and car repair so you can save some money and/or hopefully buy yourself some time before you take it in for repair.

That's why auto shop classes were invented!

Whether you're a guy or girl, **whether you're interested in working on cars or not, take auto shop.** It will be one of the most beneficial classes you ever attend (typing is another one). You'll find plenty of use your whole life for what you learn. (How many classes can you actually say that about?)

Learn how to MANAGE your money.

Making a budget and keeping up with it will come in handy when you have a family. But why wait till then? It can improve your life right now! Check out what Todd Temple has to say.

HOW TO HANDLE HOARDS OF CASH

Okay, maybe you're rich. **Maybe you have a million dollars in the bank**—a Swiss bank. Maybe your baseball card collection or your Precious Moments collection is worth $17,000; you're not sure, exactly, because your butler takes care of it for you.

And maybe your stereo has 200 watts of power, dual tape decks, and a CD changer that also plays laser disks on the big-screen TV, *and* it's a Walkman! Instead of watching *Home Improvement* reruns after school, you take your personal jet to British Columbia to go heli-skiing. (Sure, you bring along a couple of friends, but you put dibs on the front seat.)

And maybe you hide the money in a sock, which is inside a box underneath the right-hand bottom drawer of your dresser. Of course, everyone does this, but you're the only one with $2,000 in his sock.

Maybe you're that rich.

Probably not. If you're like most teens, you're not even dreaming of a million dollars—you'd be happy to save your first hundred. That can be a tough thing to do.

Every day, a thousand times a day, **people tell you what to do with your money.** And they're saying the same thing: SPEND IT.

Virtually every TV commercial, radio spot, billboard, and magazine ad is saying it. The people who make shoes and shirts and skis and stereos and sunglasses and snacks and super-cheeseburgers spend billions of dollars in advertising each year to get you to spend your money on their stuff.

Well, I'd like to help you out. If I had the money, I'd hire a music superstar and do a hot commercial where he tells you how cool it is to save. I'd put billboards that say STICK IT IN THE BANK! I'd run magazine ads that show a beautiful woman hugging a guy who's wearing cheap, no-name shoes. (The caption: "And she doesn't even care about my shoes!")

But I don't have a million dollars. So instead of advertising the message, I'll just tell you right now. Here's some simple money-saving advice that will help you get your first hundred—and the second hundred, and the third . . . **as far as you want to go.**

INVEST IN THINGS THAT GO UP

It sounds obvious, but most people don't. You see, every time you spend money, **you're making an investment.** And what you spend it on either goes up or down in value. The moment you buy a shirt or stereo or movie rental or fast-food meal, you lose money. That's because you can never sell these things for as much as you paid for them ("slightly used Chicken McNuggets for sale, best offer").

But if you "spent" that $5 or $10 or $50 at the bank, you could get it back with interest. Banks are good "up" investments. Another good "up" is buying something that will help you make more money. Buy a snow shovel, tool kit, lawn mower, or computer—then clear driveways, fix bikes, mow lawns, or type reports for others.

People who save money are good at saying no to "downs." Say no to your $5-a-week fast-food investment and put that money in the bank instead. By summer you'll have over $100.

INVEST IN PAIRS

It's hard to save money when your friends aren't. They get to order milk shakes . . . you get to chew on a straw. They load video games with quarters . . . you beg to play their bonus rounds. They go to the movies . . . you go shopping with your little sister for her piano recital dress. Oh, to be a spender again!

There's another way. **Get a friend to save with you.** Set a goal together, like saving $10 each week. Go to the bank every Monday after school to deposit your weekend earnings, then hang around together the rest of the week so you'll have someone to chew straws with. Better yet, **come up with fun stuff to do that doesn't involve money.** Go running, build an igloo, invent a new language, learn to juggle, pin your sister's doll collection to the ceiling. Cheap thrills.

INVEST EVERY WEEK

"If only I had a hundred dollars . . . then I'd be able to start saving for something." Lots of people don't save money because they don't have any money to save. (So they say.)

Even if you scrounge up just a few dollars a week from allowance or dog walking or cruising pay phones, you can take something to the bank. You're only going to make more money as time goes on. **Now is the time to create a habit of investing** in an "up" each week.

You may not have a cool million, a butler, and a jet. But you're still rich.

That's because you can spend whatever money you *do* have on whatever you want.

With no rent, no insurance, no utilities, and no car payment, **you're the envy of the adult world!**

Your freedom with money—and freedom from it—will end in a few years.

So my best advice is, enjoy it! Have fun with your money. Spend it on good stuff. Learn to save some of it each week. And **give some of it back to God as a way of saying thanks** for whatever you have. That's the biggest "up" of all.

(Excerpted from the 1992 January issue of Breakaway *magazine.)*

Facts and Pretty Worthless Information About Money

• In 1989, **the president of Disney earned over $50 million** (that's about $16,000 an hour).

• All the gold ever mined in the world would fit inside one oil tanker.

• Americans spend $7 billion a year on funerals and burials.

• Nearly half of all U.S. teenagers own their own TV.

• **In 1950, the minimum wage was 75 cents an hour.**

• The largest U.S. bill ever was a $100,000 note.

• The largest bill now is $100.

• George Washington never threw a silver dollar across the Potomac— they didn't make them back then.

• Manhattan was first bought for $34 in beads. The land value is now about $17 billion.

• It's illegal to print a color picture of U.S. currency.

• **"One," as numeral or word, appears 16 times on a U.S. dollar bill.**

• The average life of a dollar bill is 12 to 18 months.

WHERE TO FIND MONEY

•Beneath couch cushions after big people with pockets have sat there. (Best to wait until after they get up.)

.Under the check-out counter at the supermarket.

•Near phone booths where business people in suits drop coins but won't pick them up because it's not worth soiling their expensive outfits.

•In a bank vault (but it's best to leave it there).

.Beneath the fast-food drive-thru window on a wet day when people with shivering hands fumble their change but don't want to open the car door and get their sleeves dirty by brushing them against the mud on the bottom of the car door.

•Anywhere below a helicopter that happens to be dumping dollar bills onto a city. **(Safety tip: If it's dumping quarters, wear a helmet.)**

TIPS FOR COMPULSIVE SPENDERS

·Ask why. Before you fork over cash, ask yourself, "Why do I want this thing?" If you can't come up with a good reason, put it back.

·Count to seven. Live by the seven-over-seven rule: Anytime you want to spend over seven dollars on something, wait seven days for it. This "cooling off" period will help you decide whether you really want it.

·Don't save by spending. Walk away when someone says a deal is "too good to pass up" or "you'll never find as good a deal as this." **You'll always find a better deal.** Even if the deal is incredible. Investing in an "up" is an even better one. (When the check-out clerk at a discount store tells me I just saved three dollars by shopping there, I tell him I didn't save anything—I just spent fifteen.)

·Write it down. Every time you spend money on something, write it down. Just the trouble of recording the purchase will remind you of how much money you spend on silly things. This is "aversion therapy"—the same as when adults attempt to alter your behavior by making you write a hundred times ("I will not pin my little sister's doll collection to the ceiling . . . I will not pin my little sister's doll collection . . . ")

·Keep it at home. Figure out exactly how much money you'll need that day and put that much in your wallet. Leave the rest hidden at home . . . in that place you think no one knows about, but your mom discovered four years ago.

47 You're not GUARANTEED a middle-class income because you're a Christian

This one seems like a no-brainer, but you'd be surprised how many Christians feel that if God doesn't give them a high measure of prosperity, He must not be too special. **We Americans are spoiled,** selfish, and unfortunately, come with tons of wrong expectations about what it means to have God's blessing on our lives.

When taken in its proper perspective, money is fine. It gives you more options and affords you the chance to be a bigger giver to God's work. But having a moderate to huge bank account isn't a promise from Scripture. In fact, Jesus said it's easier to put a camel through the eye of a needle than for a rich man to enter the Kingdom of heaven. Riches have a way of transferring your trust in the unseen to a trust in what you can see. And in our money-conscious world, where dollars bring a measure of security and pleasure, **it's tempting to forget about God if the dollars are there.**

If you work hard and smart in life, and God chooses to give you more money than most (not "bless" you with more money), just realize this privilege comes with bigger responsibilities—and hassles. God is very selective about whom He entrusts with riches, and even Christian rich people who are selected for wealth don't always act right once they have it.

Contentment is the key word. Pursue your goals and dream big if you want, but **keep your expectations of yourself and God realistic.** Remember, it's the LOVE of money that is the root of all sorts of evil, not money itself (1 Timothy 6:10).

48} It's OKAY to be afraid.

Everyone's afraid of *something*. I (Susie) am afraid of being on a train that derails. And bugs—**I'm really scared of bugs.** *Yeeeech!* And a grand piano falling from a thirty-two-story building while I'm walking by scares me. I'm also frightened of being captured by aliens and being forced to do math homework for years on end, and forgetting to brush my teeth and having bad breath all day, and falling out of a Ferris wheel and getting rabies just because I feed carrots to the stray rabbits that wander in and out of my neighborhood, and being run over while I'm riding my moped, and forgetting to change clothes and going to work in my pajamas. I'm scared of lots of stuff!

While it's okay to be afraid once in a while, it's *not* okay to let our fears take the best of us. For instance, if you don't have many friends because you're *afraid* to MAKE any friends, then fear is robbing you of an important part of life.

Determine to overcome!

When a fear grows bigger and larger in our minds, we become obsessed with it. And when an obsessive fear gets out of control, it becomes a phobia.

Well-known author and public Christian speaker, Patsy Clairmont, admits she used to be *agoraphobic*—she was afraid to leave her home and go out in public. This fear became so much a part of her life that she finally realized something was terribly wrong. She was allowing her fear to rob her of many blessings, as well as keeping her from **the adventure of meeting new people** and traveling to new places. With God's help, she overcame it and now travels all across the United States communicating His love to large groups of people.

Here are a few phobias you may not be aware of: *hematophobia* (sight of blood), *monophobia* (being alone), *ombrophobia* (rain), *erthyrophobia* (blushing in public), *anthophobia* (flowers), *phonophobia* (speaking aloud), *toxophobia* (being poisoned), *trichophobia* (hair).

While you probably don't suffer from any of the above, **you might be allowing fear to rob you of something terrific.** For instance, could it be that the reason you're not growing spiritually is because you're afraid of what God *might* ask of you? Do you avoid opposite sex friendships because you're scared of not knowing what to say or how to act? What about witnessing? **Are you afraid that others will make fun of you?**

Why not take a few minutes right now and ask God to reveal to you any fears that are holding you back from becoming all He wants you to be. Once you've identified what you're afraid of, jot them down on a piece of paper. Now, **commit those fears to God.** Tell Him you want ALL that He has in store for you. Refuse to let *any* fear stand between you and your Creator.

"My chosen ones, don't be afraid" (Isaiah 44:2b, TLB).

Some people CHEAT and get away with it.

But you've already noticed this, right?

Kids are cheating in school all the time. Maybe *you've* even done it and have gotten away with it. Since it didn't really hurt anyone, **you may be tempted to keep it up.** (Others in school certainly are.)

What we've seen is that those who start young and cheat in the little things usually continue cheating later in life, but this time in bigger things. **Some are in jail because of it.** Most aren't. They took "short cuts" to get through their education, they "borrow" from their employer, and they "fudge" a little on their taxes. They think that whatever advantage they can get that doesn't directly "hurt" someone else is okay. Where did this line of thinking start? When they were kids, of course.

Our point isn't to repeat what we talked about in *Lockers, Lunch Lines, Chemistry, and Cliques*, but rather to let you see the bigger picture: If you start young with anything—good or bad—you're likely to continue that habit as you progress through life.

Cheating is occurring all around you by people of weak character who can't face the consequences of their own limitations.

Don't be weak.

Have a strong character.

Face the consequences of your actions like a Christian soldier.

Realize you do have limitations.

Don't try to overcome them by cheating. **Just work harder.**

Newspapers don't ALWAYS print the truth.

You've probably heard it said that **"Just because it's in black-and-white doesn't make it true."**

Well, if you've seen *that* statement in black-and-white, IT *IS* TRUE!

Newspapers, magazines, movie companies, textbook publishers, radio and TV stations—all are businesses owned by people—people whose spin on life doesn't necessarily come from the Bible. That means it could come from any-where (and usually does).

So if *USA Today* runs an article loaded with tons of statistics that *prove* pedophiles (people who sexually abuse small children), adulterers (people who cheat on their spouse), or homosexuals have a gene that makes them that way (yes, they've actually printed this), take it with a grain of salt.

Key point! Don't get the idea that **everything** in print has a hid-den anti-Christian message behind it. That's obviously not the case. But it *is* important to think about what you're reading or watching, compare it to the truth of the Bible, check the facts, and decide for yourself. **Be a respon- sible reader!**

HOLLYWOOD is more about making money and "artistic expression" than producing quality entertainment.

Will the crowds line up to see the movie? Will they flock to see it in Tokyo and London? Are there hot merchandising possibilities (products that tie in to the movie)? How well will it sell at the corner home-video store?

These and other questions all revolve around the bottom line: **money.** Like any other business, if the product won't make money, it doesn't get made. If Hollywood execs doubt anyone will shell out hard cash to see a film, it isn't too likely to be produced.

Naturally, movie studios would rather produce a good film than a bad one, but that isn't necessarily their primary goal. Most studios want first to produce what they think will sell. If producers and writers determine that audiences want swearing, violence, and sex (which, to various degrees, all PG-13 and R-rated movies contain), then that's what will receive production dollars.

"Artistic expression" is usually a secondary goal for making movies. Though sales figures have shown that family-oriented movies make money, few producers are making them. Why? They want to make movies that **make some kind of statement**—usually a moral, social, or political one. Does the typical Hollywood statement reflect biblical values? Not usually!

Movies *can* be great entertainment as well as a powerful force to change the hearts and minds of those who watch them. But **be careful about what you buy.** Read reviews, talk to friends and people whose opinions you respect. Do a little homework to see if the picture you're planning to see is really something you will enjoy—and feel good about afterward.

Ditto for TV—only with a FEW exceptions.

As with movies, TV shows, whether they're thirty-minute sitcoms or one-hour dramas, only air if a studio can line up enough sponsors to make money. If the show doesn't get high ratings, the advertising dollars go down. That's when a show goes off the air—whether it's quality entertainment or not.

For major network shows, advertising dollars determine what is on your tube. Period. And advertisers can't afford to back shows with smaller audiences.

Cable TV, however, can offer more quality options than regular TV because **there are so many channels available,** and each can focus on a narrower audience. Also, many cable channels aren't solely dependent on advertisers for income. They get an agreed-upon amount for each home that orders the channel. That means their programming still has to attract viewers, or cable companies will drop it from their line-up, but it doesn't have to attract top-dollar from advertisers. *The Family Channel* is a perfect example of a network with a mission to put on quality shows that still makes a nice profit.

The reason we even mention TV is that **most people blindly ingest what they're being fed** from the "tube." The same thinking that says, "If it's in print, it must be true" affects what people believe about TV—and movies: "If it's on the screen, it must be okay."

To survive on Planet Earth you must be someone who DISCERNS the good from the bad. And **after you determine what isn't quality, avoid it!**

Learn to HEAR God's voice.

What does *that* have to do with surviving Planet Earth? A LOT. If you can hear His voice above the shuffling of feet in your high school hallway, the scrunching of paper in your classroom, the screaming and clapping on your football field, the blaring of horns and screeching of brakes on your city streets . . . then you'll be able to hear His voice *anywhere*.

And we think **that's pretty important,** because fifteen years from now, when you're in a full-time career and making decisions in a boardroom, **you'll need to hear His voice.**

Listen.

Really listen.

You'll be amazed at what you hear!

54} It's OKAY to cry.

When *you're* hurting, God hurts. He feels the pain *with* you. And while He never promises to take the pain away, He DOES promise strength to make it *through* the pain.

So go ahead.

Have a good cry.

It's okay. Really.

55} NO ONE looks as good in real life as on TV.

Even Cindy Crawford says it takes an entire crew *hours* to get her to look "casual." And every magazine cover in the WORLD has been touched up and perfected. Working on *Brio* and *Breakaway* magazines has taught us that it's fairly easy to make ANYONE look good because photos can be easily "fixed."

With the stroke of a few computer keys, bags are removed from underneath the eyes, teeth are whitened, sunburns are replaced with tans, and zits disappear.

So the next time you oooh and ahhhh over someone in print, think twice. **They're not perfect.** And if you think you have to live up to someone's false image, you're listening to the father of lies—Satan himself.

Some things are WORTH fighting for.

Others aren't.

Learn the difference.

57} LEARN to cook five meals and wash your own clothes.

You don't have to be a gourmet, you don't have to be Mom, you don't even have to come close to being Grandma. But if you know how to cook five meals (TV dinners don't count), **you'll probably keep yourself alive.** Here are a few easy ones:

- Spaghetti with meatballs

- Hamburgers

- Fried chicken with rice and green vegetable

- Teriyaki stir-fry vegetables

- Omelets of all shapes, sizes, and ingredients

Keep track of all of the meals you know how to cook, and expand the list as often as you can. **Cooking is actually a pretty fun thing to do.** And when you start dating or get married, it's even more enjoyable to cook together.

As for laundry, just learn how to do these different types of clothes and **you'll be set for life:**

- whites

- delicates

- darks (jeans, etc.)

- sweaters

- permanent press

You can be your own BEST FRIEND ... or your own WORST ENEMY.

Ways to be your own best friend:

•Believe what God says about you.

•Hang out with people who have your best interests at heart, who build you up and don't tear you down, who tell you the truth.

•Try to become friends with your parents.

•Serve others whenever possible.

•Stay physically active, eat right, and get the right amount of sleep.

•Develop the habit of talking to God throughout the day.

•Work hard.

•Play hard—and relax when you can.

•Keep your expectations realistic.

•Whatever you do in life, don't do it halfway. Like your mom said, "If something is worth doing, it's worth doing well."

Want to be your own worst enemy? Just do the opposite of each of these.

Let Jesus REMOLD you.

Even though we're all created in God's image, because we're born stubborn, we often venture off on our own and demand our rights. That's exactly what Sam did. (Okay, that wasn't his *real* name, but we're never told what his real name was. He's the runaway in the story of the Prodigal Son.) It's all found in Luke 15:11–32.

You're probably familiar with the confrontation between father and son. But **for a quick recap,** let's take a peek at how the conversation began:

"Father, give me my share of the estate" (v. 12, NIV).

Notice what demand stands out: GIVE ME! That's the heart of all rebellion, isn't it? It's the same thing as saying to our heavenly Father, "I don't care that you created me in your image. I'm gonna be my own person, and I'm gonna do my own thing."

Give me. I want my own way.

Well, you know the story. The father lets him go, and the son becomes involved in all kinds of rebellious activity. By the time he's ready to come back, he's had a **complete change of heart.** He's learned that **his father really knows what's best for him.** Sam admits he was wrong and humbles himself before his dad.

Let's listen in on the conversation *now.*

" . . . Father, I have sinned against heaven and against you. I am no longer worthy to be called your son; make me like one of your hired men" (vv. 18–19, NIV).

NOW notice what stands out: MAKE ME! That's the cry of a broken heart that can be molded and reshaped by Jesus Christ.

Where are *you?* Demanding your rights? Those who are busy screaming "Give me!" are so caught up in making demands that they have forgotten how to kneel and quietly plead, "Make me."

"Make me, Jesus. Make me. **Break me and reshape me.** Mold me in your image."

Ask your parents LOTS of questions.

After you've talked about their relationship with Christ and their relationship with each other, ask them to teach you about practical stuff that you'll need to know in order to be successful in life.

One of the most important things to learn is how to create a budget and live within it. Ask them to show you *their* budget. If you act interested enough, they may let you in on how they pay bills and still manage to save a little for emergencies. **Why is this boring stuff so important for a teen?**

It'll come in REAL handy when you're trying to pay apartment rent, treat your date to a special evening, make ends meet in college, and still have enough change to do laundry.

A few more important things to ask your folks? Try these topics:

•What do you believe about heaven and hell?

•How do I apply for things like a car loan, credit cards, or a house loan?

•How can I establish good credit without taking *out* too much credit?

•What do you believe about euthanasia?

•Have you made out a will?

•For what would I need to use a notary public?

•(List a few questions of your own that you want to be sure to cover.)

61. Sunday afternoon naps really DO make a difference.

There's nothing better than to come home from church, eat a big dinner, lie in front of the TV and watch a football game . . . and fall asleep on the couch.

There's nothing better than to take a good book into your room, ask not to be disturbed . . . and head off into dreamland for an hour or so with the book still in your hands.

You'll feel great for the rest of the day.

Try it!

Learn to make people feel SPECIAL.

This takes time, but it sure makes a BIG difference. Jot a few notes during the week (not just to your best friends, but maybe even to an old grade school friend), make some calls, **remember birthdays.** People will start to believe you really care. And if they believe you really care about them (which you do, of course), **they'll probably start really caring for you.** Life becomes exceedingly worthwhile when you know people really care.

But don't expect *someone else* to care unless YOU care.

Who you are in public has a LOT to do with who you are in private (even though we all try to pretend it doesn't).

It's easy to be considerate, patient, and generous when everyone's watching.

But when the spotlight's off and you're all alone, or just with your family, are you the same person?

Remember this: **No one can maintain a false image forever.** Sooner or later, everyone will see the "real you."

64} Read BETWEEN the lines when a friend cuts you off or blows up at you.

Your first reaction will be "Sheesh! What'd I do?" **Most of the time it's not you at all**, it's something going on inside of him. Maybe he just blew a test, had a fight with his parents, his gerbil is deathly ill (or worse yet, his golden retriever), he just discovered he's got two different color socks on, his P.E. teacher made fun of his new sneakers, he found out he needs glasses, he didn't make the football team. . . . As you can see, a million different tragedies could have occurred, so when he blows up at you, he's actually blowing up at life. **Don't take it personally.**

Put a garbage bag in your car so you WON'T be tempted to toss trash out the window.

And by the way, **when you see trash on the ground, take time to pick it up.** You'll never regret you did because you'll be helping to make Planet Earth a much prettier place to live.

Drive-thrus aren't always the QUICKEST or best way to get a bag of fries.

Oh sure, it may *seem* faster, but **how many times have you had to repeat your order?** How many times have you dropped money trying to pay for it—or trying to get your change? (And then it was too cold or too rainy to bother getting out and retrieving it.) How many times have they gotten your order wrong and you didn't find out until you were four miles away; then it was too late to go back because you were late for something?

So you see, **quicker is not always better.**

67. Don't get CARRIED away.

It's easy to get **caught up in the moment** and take something too far. Say you're going to the grocery store to get some microwave popcorn and soft drinks because your friends are coming over later to watch *The Santa Clause*—even though it's July. (You're creative—see chapter 2.)

You notice **a good-looking guy** (guys, you can change this to girl, but since I'm writing it (Susie) I'm gonna use guy, okay?) about two hundred feet in front of you. He's rounding the corner of the aisle you're entering, so you hurry and catch up with him. Well, you stay at least eight inches behind him so he won't suspect you're observing and following him—and you notice he has some Lean Cuisine frozen meals in his cart, so you immediately know that **he's health conscious.** (And he's not wearing a wedding ring.) You grab a couple of Weight Watcher meals with one hand and guide your cart in his direction with your other hand as you notice him eyeing a bag of potato chips. Alex (that's what you're calling him now in your thoughts) reads the back of the package carefully, so you surmise he's cautious about fat grams, calories, and ingredients. You like that—a lot. Because **you're cautious,** too. You'd never use that fake, fat-laden cool-whipped topping. Uh-uh. Nothing but the real stuff for you. He puts the chips down and grabs a bag of pretzels. You grin because now you know he's a Monopoly player. After all, your family used to play Monopoly every Sunday night after church while eating pretzels, too. You're glad **you already have so much in common** with Brandon (Alex seemed too "old," so you switched names). He picks up two apples, a bag of carrots, three grapefruit, and some snow peas—and even though you don't really like fruits and vegetables, you're crazy about Chinese food, and what entree doesn't contain those little snow peas! **You're dreaming** about having Chinese food together—mostly sweet-and-sour pork, fortune cookies, and egg rolls . . . with a couple of snow peas mixed in somewhere, when you realize he's moved away from the fruits and veggies aisle and is heading toward the checkout stands. **You follow – I mean, observe him** entering lane #4, and you fall into line behind him. You're standing so close, you can't help but notice his clean hair and fabric of his T-shirt and the scent of his cologne! *Eternity*, you think, because you smelled that once at a Michael W. Smith concert, and you remember reading in a back issue of *Brio* magazine that that's the kind of cologne Smitty wears.

He pays cash—for all $4.79 worth of groceries—and you admire the fact that he's not abusing his charge card or writing bogus checks. You notice he gets into a smooth, shiny VW convertible bug with a great wax job, and you follow him until he pulls up in front of a large mansion. Your eyes roll to the back of your head and you think, *Oh, wow! We have soooo much in common. I clean mansions, and he lives in one!* **It's almost too much for one day.** But you get out of your car and sneak around to the front gate. Two hours later, when you've unplugged the electric fence and have given the guard dogs fresh steaks, you climb over and enter through an open window in the back.

The wooden floors are so shiny and pretty, you think for a moment you're in a bowling alley. You wander down the hallway into his bedroom. His closet door is open, so you go inside (it's one of those huge walk-ins that's about a block long).

Just then, Victor **(Brandon sounded too preppy)** enters his room singing at the top of his lungs. You want to join in, but you don't recognize the tune, so instead you just tap your feet and snap your fingers. And this is what you're doing when he opens his closet door and sees you standing there all bunchy in your sweats.

"Hi, Mort," you say (Victor had too many syllables). He doesn't say a word, but turns around lickety-split and pushes a buzzer by the side of the door. Two armed guards rush in and carry you off to the police station where you're thrown in jail with someone who made big bucks telling grade school children that it's okay to eat paste.

Somehow—it's a miracle—the police let you off with a large fine, which you were able to pay because you'd just cashed your check for cleaning houses, and they let you go. But your car is still at Jason's house (Mort sounded too old). So you call a cab, and when you get home, your friends are starting to arrive for your *Santa Clause* party. Only they're not smiling because you forgot to get the microwave popcorn and soft drinks and no one wants to eat Weight Watchers frozen diet dinners when watching *The Santa Clause.* So your friends all leave, and you never hear from them again.

If only you hadn't gotten so carried away!

68 Being open and honest is IMPORTANT, but there's a time and place for everything.

True friends will let you know when you have something in your teeth after lunch, something worse hanging out of your nose on a cold day, or your fly is open after . . . you know. (All this in private, not announced in a LOUD voice to everyone within a mile.)

They'll be open and honest when you've hurt them (or someone else) by something you've said. And when your behavior is heading off the deep end, they won't be afraid to look you in the eye and say so.

They're honest. They care. They speak up in the right way at the right time.

But do you need total openness from everyone all the time? More important, do you need to be totally honest ALL the time? Do you need to tell your best friend about the zit on her nose the size of Maine? (Like she doesn't know already.) Do you need to tell the substitute teacher about his weight problem? Do you need to tell that insecure, unpopular kid you hardly know that if he just washed his hair once a week, he'd have more friends? (Well, maybe, but get to know him first.)

Do you see the difference? **Honesty that helps is always appropriate.** Honesty that hurts, that is said wrongly or at the wrong time, isn't a good honesty.

There's a difference.

Be honest, but be careful how you pass it out.

Life won't ALWAYS make sense.

It seems unfair that school officials suddenly realigned the districts in your city, and now you're riding a bus to a school full of students you don't even know.

And why did your mom have to develop multiple sclerosis? Or why did Dad lose his job right after Thanksgiving, and you had the worst Christmas of your life? **Your girl/boyfriend broke up for some no-good reason** that you couldn't even understand, and you're failing history because your regular teacher is out on maternity leave, and you can't even understand the substitute, who talks too fast and expects too much.

It's not fair!

But **much of life is unfair.** Though your friends may not understand, there is One who does. "The Lord is close to those whose hearts are breaking" (Psalm 34:18a, TLB).

Go ahead.

Sit in His lap.

Cry on His shoulders.

It's okay.

It's okay to have a MESSY room— as long as your life isn't messy, too.

I (Susie) clean my office about five times a year . . . usually when inanimate objects start coming to life and chasing my office mates down the hallway. Other employees have impeccable work stations but aren't really that organized.

You see, **organization doesn't always mean having everything in a labeled file folder.** Many creative people are messy, but it's not really an important issue unless it spills into their lifestyle.

You can become really neat and superorganized and have an unbalanced life. You can also be extremely creative, spontaneous, and fun, and have an unbalanced life. You see, the IMPORTANT thing is not how organized you are, but whether or not your life is balanced.

Jesus is the equilibrium. Make Him the very hub around which the spokes (interests) of your life revolve. As long as He is the center of your life, it probably won't matter that you've stashed a few dirty socks under your bed. (Unless they start to smell when your dad has his boss over for dinner and he casually tours the house and faints when he walks into *your* room, and your dad gets fired because the boss cracked his head on your ski pole when he went crashing down on top of your dirty laundry. THEN it's time to clean up, pick up, and straighten up. No one likes to be sued.)

71 Don't use your car to GET EVEN.

Two times in the last three years in our medium-sized Colorado city, a ticked-off driver has been killed. That's right, *killed.*

A seventeen-year-old kid tailgated an elderly man on the freeway one sunny afternoon. When the old guy pulled over, unfortunately so did the kid. The teenager rushed out of his car to vent his anger. **They had some words,** then he punched the old guy. The old guy pulled out a gun and shot him point-blank in the chest. A seventeen-year-old *churchgoing teenage boy* with his whole life ahead of him lay dead on the freeway. (P.S. The old guy was acquitted!)

Not long afterward, two drivers in rush-hour traffic got in each other's way. Both took it personally. By the time their anger had played out, one had run the other off the road. Another human being was dead—and for no good reason. (P.S. The other guy was convicted of manslaughter and sent to prison.)

Rule 1 for driving: *This world is filled with bad drivers.*

Sometimes they're older people trying to maintain a normal life by keeping their license. Sometimes they're people who just aren't paying attention to the business of driving, or who aren't "aggressive" enough to make a left-hand turn you would have made. But most of the time **bad drivers are overaggressive, immature people whose ego takes over their brain** when they get behind the wheel.

Rule 2: *You can't change rule #1.* All you can do is decide ahead of

time how you're going to respond when you encounter an aggressive driver, or a driver with poor skills. Your response might not make the difference between life and death . . . but it could.

Being a bad driver doesn't make you a bad person.

Calling the driver ahead of you an idiot or a jerk may make you feel better temporarily, but it's probably not the truth. Having poor driving skills is not a character flaw. True, many drivers should go back to driving school to take a refresher course, but most are just doing what they were taught: driving defensively (versus offensively).

When you're driving, you can send a message to other drivers as clearly as if you had a cell phone: respect or disrespect, maturity or immaturity. It's your choice. "Do to others as you would have them do to you" (Luke 6:31, NIV) is the golden rule of life AND driving. **You're going to make mistakes behind the wheel — lots of them.** You'll want others to cut you some slack, so do the same for them. Don't use the car as a vehicle to lash out at other people, okay?

Your pet WILL die someday.

When I (Susie) was growing up, Shep was the best friend I had. He was short and stocky and had a flat head. We never knew what kind of dog he was—just that he was very special. The vet told us that **Shep was the only dog he'd ever seen who could wag his tail seven different ways.**

We got Shep when he was two and I was one. **We grew up together.** He was terrific. But when I was sixteen and he was seventeen, he died. The void he left was indescribable.

Several years later I got another dog, Goldie. She was smart, *really* smart—and protective. When a door-to-door salesman walked up my driveway to talk to me while I was standing in my garage, Goldie firmly planted herself between me and the stranger. Even though I *tried* to get around her (so I could talk face-to-face with the guy), she wouldn't let me. She maintained a low, no-messin'-around growl until the man finally left. When she was only four years old, she died, and I thought the hurt would never heal.

Then Jamaica Jane came into my life. She was two and knew all kinds of tricks. She could get my mail, catch an ice cube in midair, and even brought in the newspaper. (Problem was, I didn't subscribe to the newspaper—but she brought me all the neighbors' papers!) She was terrific! But she died when she was only five.

It hurts when a pet dies. And every time I get a *new* one, I'm faced with the decision of even getting one at all. *It's just gonna die in a few years,*

I think to myself. *Should I even get one?* We're constantly weighing the cost of hurt, aren't we?

Yet, I continue to get pet after pet because I LOVE the time I *do* have with them. I'm convinced that, even though the pain is tremendous when they die, the love and enjoyment I get from their lives—though often short-lived—makes it all worthwhile.

If you have a pet, don't take it for granted. Enjoy your time together. Take lots of pictures. **Buy some special treats once in a while.** And when your pet dies, flash back to the good times and concentrate on the positive.

Coveting: It's just NEVER worth it.

Heather *loved* Crystal's new sweater. Even though Crystal sat three rows and five chairs over, Heather just couldn't take her eyes off the sweater all during biology class.

It looks GREAT, Heather thought. *I've GOT to get one just like it!* It was all she thought about day and night for two weeks. Every time she passed Crystal in the hall, Heather felt a pang of jealousy in her heart. *It's not right that SHE gets to have such a cool sweater, and I don't,* she told herself.

So even though she'd been saving for her youth group's summer missions trip, she raided her savings account and bought the sweater.

Heather broke one of the Ten Commandments: "Thou shalt not covet."

There's a good reason God told us not to covet.

He knew coveting would get the best of us. You see, when we covet something that a neighbor or friend has, it means we want it so badly that we become obsessive about it. When we're obsessive about *anything*, it quickly becomes first place in our lives, and **Jesus is automatically pushed to second or third place.**

When you find yourself coveting something that another person has, stop immediately and begin praying. The God who told you not to do it is the same God who will bring you through it!

Don't be AFRAID of your weaknesses.

Zacchaeus wasn't. Remember him? You can get the full story in Luke 19:1-10. He was short. *So* short that people called him names. Stuff like: PeeWee, Shortstuff, Dwarfo, Turtle, Baby, Little Guy (they weren't real creative with these names, were they?), Microscopic, Minnie, Germ, Molecule, Pinhead, and Bob.

He grew up with these names. **He knew what it was like to always be picked last when dividing into teams.** He'd been pushed to the back of the lunch line more times than he could count. And he was so little that once in a while someone wouldn't even notice he was sitting in a chair, and they'd sit right on top of him!

But Zack didn't let being short stop him. The scene: Jesus was coming to Zack's city—Jericho. People had come out EN MASSE to see Him. They lined all the streets and even filled up the parking lots.

Everyone wanted a glimpse—including Zack. But he couldn't see two feet in front of him. He was just too short. He *could* have given up. He *could* have thought, *Oh, well. I tried to see Him. Guess I'll never get to meet Jesus. I'm just too short.*

But instead of giving in to his shortcoming, he did something about it. He climbed a tree! Not only did Zack see Jesus, but **Jesus saw Zack!** The rest is history. Jesus called him by name (don't you love it when your heavenly Father calls you by name!) and motioned for him to come down. They walked away and headed for Zack's house.

And you know what? Zack was never seen as *short* again!

All of us have limitations. Weaknesses. Failures.

Instead of denying them, ignoring them, or trying to cover them up, **why not just admit it?** That's what Zack did. *Yep, I'm short,* he thought. *Guess I'd better do something about it if I'm gonna see Jesus.*

That's the key: Doing something about it! You're not good at math? Get some tutoring. Have a problem making friends? Start with reaching out to just one. Got a smart mouth? Ask your parents to hold you accountable.

Since we all have shortcomings, we all have two choices: **We can either let our shortcomings get the best of us, or we can rise above them.**

Create a Zack-A-Tude. Create an attitude like Zacchaeus, and do something about it!

Being a Christian is probably the BEST thing in the whole world.

The Newsboys wrote a song a while back that had these lyrics as the main part of the song.

When we don't get what we deserve, it's a real good thing. A real good thing.

When we get what we don't deserve, it's a real good thing. A real good thing.

Besides with our parents, perhaps, there aren't too many places these two phrases apply.

But if we've asked Jesus Christ into our lives, then we don't get hell—something we deserve. And because we're children of the KING, He lavishes on us blessings abundant. We don't deserve them, but He gives them to us anyway.

That's a real good thing.

76} PSSST! It never pays to gossip!

"Did you hear that Troy likes Erika? I promised I wouldn't tell anyone, but . . .well, *you're* not *anyone*, so it's probably okay."

"Wow. I didn't know that! But **guess what I heard?** Mrs. James, the math teacher, came to school with a black eye. I heard a girl in the bathroom say she thinks Mrs. James' husband beats her!"

Gossip is something you just can't win at. It *always* hurts, and **it always comes back to you.** When was the last time *you* gossiped? When was the last time you *listened* to gossip? Whether you're spreading it or listening to it is all the same in God's eyes. And He *abhors* it. (That means He hates it with a passion!)

Why not take a few minutes right now to refresh your mind on what James has to say about the tongue (James, chapter 1).

Pretty powerful stuff, huh? The next time you get the itch to participate in gossip, **send an S.O.S. prayer** to God instead. Only He can help you put an end to the ugly gossip habit.

Make it your goal to MASTER the Bible.

After high school, when I (Greg) first became a Christian, I borrowed an older Revised Standard Version of the Bible from home. I read about a paragraph once every other night. My problem was that I really didn't understand the RSV very well. Somehow it was intimidating. Plus, I didn't have anyone to show me *what* to read. **Though I knew I should read God's Word, I avoided it.** That summer, a friend gave me *The Living Bible* version of the New Testament. The print was bigger, the lines more widely spaced . . . I could read it without getting a headache! And that's what I did. In my spare time I'd sit and read twenty chapters at a time, day after day. When I finished, I started over. I couldn't get enough! That summer **I learned to love and appreciate God's Word.** I wasn't spending time with a book; I was spending time at the feet of Jesus.

I had a deep hunger to know more about God and the Bible, so while attending a secular university, I signed up for a Bible class at the local Christian college. It was so good I transferred to that school and took a double major: psychology and biblical studies. It was the best decision I ever made. It gave me a foundation for life that is still serving me today.

Very few people become *extremely* knowledgeable about anything: a sport, hobby, or subject in school. A few, however, know that if you want to get ahead and be the best you can possibly be, you have to pursue becoming a master of at least one thing. We challenge you to make it your lifetime goal to

become a master of the Bible.

Because people have differing views of the Bible and what it means, we know there are hindrances to fulfilling that challenge. See if you can pick how God wants you to view the Bible:

A. A book so big that you never want to go near it.

B. Words so complicated you get confused every time you start to read.

C. History so boring its only use is as a sleeping aid.

D. Commandments so burdensome there's no point in knowing them because they can't be kept.

E. **An old friend so trustworthy you can't get enough of its wisdom.**

If you picked "E," you win a cookie.

So how do you learn to trust an old friend? You spend time with him. **Deep trust and appreciation often take years to develop.** But once you have that close friendship, you wouldn't trade it for anything else life can offer. The only way to get beyond the typical initial reactions about investing time in the Bible (and thus, with Jesus) is to persevere in the beginning stages and realize **the Bible truly can become the friend you turn to each new day.**

Planet Earth survival depends on your ability to view the Bible correctly and pursue mastering it diligently.